Second Book of Tales by Eugene Field

Eugene Field was born on 2nd September 1850 in St. Louis, Missouri. His mother died when he was six and his father when he was nineteen. His academic life was not taken seriously and he preferred the life of a prankster until, in 1875, he began work as a journalist for the St. Joseph Gazette in Saint Joseph, Missouri.

In his career as a journalist he soon found a niche that suited him. His articles were light, humorous and written in a personal gossipy style that endeared him to his readership. Some were soon being syndicated to other newspapers around the States. Field soon rose to city editor of the Gazette.

Field had first published poetry in 1879, when his poem 'Christmas Treasures' appeared. This was the beginning that would eventually number over a dozen volumes. As well as verse Field published an extensive range of short stories including 'The Holy Cross' and 'Daniel and the Devil.'

In 1889 whilst the family were in London and Field himself was recovering from a bout of ill health he wrote his most famous poem; 'Lovers Lane'.

On 4th November 1895 Eugene Field Sr died in Chicago of a heart attack at the age of 45.

Index of Contents

INTRODUCTION

Of all American poets Field, it seems to me, best understood the heart of a child. Other sweet singers have given us the homely life of the Western cabin, the unexpected tenderness of the mountaineer, the loyalty and quaint devotion of the negro servant, but to Field alone, and in preëminent degree, was given that keen insight into child nature, that compassion for its faults, that sympathy with its sorrows and that delight in its joyous innocence which will endear him to his race as long as our language is read.

His poems too always kindle afresh that spark of child life which still lies smouldering in the hearts of us all, no matter how poor and sorrowful our beginnings. As we read, how the old memories come back to us! Old hopes, rosy with the expectation of the indefinite and unknowable. Old misgivings and fears; old rompings and holidays and precious idle hours. We know them all, and we know how true they are. We remember in our own case the very hour and day, and how it all happened and why, and what came of it, joys and sorrows as real as our keenest experiences since.

This is a heritage plentiful and noble, and this heritage is Field's.

In the last paragraphs of that tender prose poem of "Bill the Lokil Editor" one of the Profitable Tales Bill "alluz fond uv children 'nd birds 'nd flowers" Bill, who was like the old sycamore that the lightning had struck, with the vines spread all around and over it, covering its scars and splintered branches occurs this passage:

"That's Bill perhaps as he stands up f'r jedgment a miserable, tremblin', 'nd unworthy thing, perhaps, but twined about, all over, with singin' and pleadin' little children and that is pleasin' in God's sight, I know."

If Field had nothing else to bring he could say truthfully as he faced his Master:

"I followed in your footsteps. I loved the children and the children loved me."

HUMIN NATUR' ON THE HAN'BUL 'ND ST. JO

Durin' war times the gorillas hed torn up most uv the cypress ties an' used 'em for kindlin' an' stove wood, an' the result wuz that when the war wuz over there wuz n't anythink left uv the Han'bul 'nd St. Jo but the rollin' stock 'nd the two streaks uv rails from one end uv the road to the other. In the spring uv '67 I hed to go out into Kansas; and takin' the Han'bul 'nd St. Jo at Palmyry Junction, I wuz n't long in findin' out that the Han'bul 'nd St. Jo railroad wuz jist about the wust cast of rollin' prairer I ever struck.

There wuz one bunk left when I boarded the sleepin' car, and I hed presence uv mind 'nuff to ketch on to it. It wuz then just about dusk, an' the nigger that sort uv run things in the car sez to me: "Boss," sez he, "I 'll have to get you to please not to snore to night, but to be uncommon quiet."

"What for?" sez I. "Hain't I paid my two dollars, an' hain't I entitled to all the luxuries uv the outfit?"

Then the nigger leant over an' told me that Colonel Elijah Gates, one uv the directors uv the road, an' the richest man in Marion County, wuz aboard, an' it wuz one uv the rules uv the company not to do anythink to bother him or get him to sell his stock.

The nigger pointed out Colonel Gates, 'nd I took a look at him as he sot readin' the "Palmyry Spectator." He wuz one of our kind uv people long, raw boned, 'nd husky. He looked to be about sixty may be not quite on to sixty. He wuz n't bothered with much hair onto his head, 'nd his beard was shaved, all except two rims or fringes uv it that ran down the sides uv his face 'nd met underneath his chin. This fringe filled up his neck so thet he did n't hev to wear no collar, 'nd he had n't no jewelry about him excep' a big carnelian bosom pin that hed the picture uv a woman's head on it in white. His specs sot well down on his nose, 'nd I could see his blue eyes over 'em small eyes, but kind ur good natured. Between his readin' uv his paper 'nd his eatin' plug terbacker he kep' toler'ble busy till come bedtime. The rest on us kep' as quiet as we could, for we knew it wuz an honor to ride in the same sleepin' car with the richest man in Marion County 'nd a director uv the Han'bul 'nd St. Jo to boot.

Along 'bout eight o'clock the colonel reckoned he 'd tumble into bed. When he 'd drawed his boots 'nd hung up his coat 'nd laid in a fresh hunk uv nat'ral leaf, he crawled into the best bunk, 'nd presently we heerd him sleepin'. There wuz nuthin' else for the rest uv us to do but to foller suit, 'nd we did.

It must have been about an hour later say along about Prairer City that a woman come aboard with a baby. There war n't no bunk for her, but the nigger allowed that she might set back near the stove, for the baby 'peared to be kind ov sick like, 'nd the woman looked like she had been cryin'. Whether it wuz the jouncin' uv the car, or whether the young one wuz hungry or hed a colic into it, I did n't know, but anyhow the train had n't pulled out uv Prairer City afore the baby began to take on. The nigger run back as fast as he could, 'nd told the young woman that she 'd have to keep that baby quiet because Colonel 'Lijy Gates, one uv the directors uv the road, wuz in the car 'nd wunt be disturbed. The young woman caught up the baby scart like, 'nd talked soothin' to it, 'nd covered its little face with her shawl, 'nd done all them things thet women do to make babies go to sleep.

But the baby would cry, and, in spite of all the young woman 'nd the nigger could do, Colonel Elijah Gates heard the baby cryin', and so he waked up. First his two blue yarn socks come through the curtains, 'nd then his long legs 'nd long body 'nd long face hove into sight. He come down the car to the young woman, 'nd looked at her over his specs. Did n't seem to be the least bit mad; jest solemn 'nd bizness like.

"My dear madam," sez he to the young woman, "you must do sumpin' to keep that child quiet. These people have all paid for their bunks, 'nd they are entitled to a good night's sleep. Of course I know how 't is with young children will cry sometimes have raised 'leven uv 'em myself, 'nd know, all about 'em. But as a director uv the Han' bul 'nd St. Jo I 've got to pertect the rights of these other folks. So jist keep the baby quiet as you kin."

Now, there war n't nothin' cross in the colonel's tone; the colonel wuz as kind 'nd consid'rit as could be expected uv a man who hed so much responsibility a restin' onto him. But the young woman was kind uv nervous, 'nd after the colonel went back 'nd got into his bunk the young woman sniffled and worrited and seemed like she had lost her wits, 'nd the baby kep' cryin' jist as hard as ever.

Waal, there wuz n't much sleepin' to be done in that car, for what with the baby cryin', 'nd the young woman a sayin', "Oh, dear!" 'nd "Oh, my!" and the nigger a prancin' round like the widder bewitched with all this goin' on, sleep wuz out uv the question. Folks began to wake up 'nd put their heads outern their bunks to see what wuz the doggone matter. This made things pleasanter for the young woman. The colonel stood it as long as he could, and then he got up a second time 'nd come down the car 'nd looked at the young woman over his specs.

"Now, as I wuz tellin' you afore," sez he, "I hain't makin' no complaint uv myself, for I 've raised a family of 'leven children, 'nd I know all about 'em. But these other folks here in the car have paid for a good night's sleep, 'nd it 's my duty as a director uv the Han'bul 'nd St. Jo to see that they get it. Seems to me like you ought to be able to keep that child quiet you can't make me believe that there's any use for a child to be carryin' on so. Sumpin 's hurtin' it I know sumpin 's hurtin' it by the way it cries. Now, you look 'nd see if there ain't a pin stickin' into it somewhere; I 've raised 'leven children, 'nd that 's jist the way they used to cry when there wuz a pin stickin' em."

He reckoned he 'd find things all right this time, 'nd he went back to his bunk feelin' toler'ble satisfied with himself. But the young woman could n't find no pin stickin' the baby, 'nd, no matter how much she stewed and worrited, the baby kep' right on cryin', jest the same. Holy smoke! but how that baby did cry.

Now, I reckoned that the colonel would be gettin' almighty mad if this thing kep' up much longer. A man may raise 'leven children as easy as rollin' off 'n a log, 'nd yet the twelfth one, that is n't his at all, may break him. There is ginerally a last straw, even when it comes to the matter uv children.

So when the colonel riz feet foremost for the third time outern his bunk that night or, I should say, mornin', for it was mighty near mornin' now we looked for hail Columby.

"Look a here, my good woman," sez he to the young woman with the baby, "as I wuz tellin' you afore, you must do sumpin to keep that child quiet. It 'll never do to keep all these folks awake like this. They 've paid for a good night's sleep, 'nd it 's my duty as a director uv the Han'bul 'nd St. Jo to pertest ag'in' this disturbance. I 've raised a family uv 'leven children, 'nd I know, as well as I know anythink, that that child is hungry. No child ever cries like that when it is n't hungry, so I insist on your nursin' it 'nd givin' us peace 'nd quiet."

Then the young woman began to sniffle.

"Law me, sir," sez the young woman, "I ain't the baby's mother I 'm only just tendin' it."

The colonel got pretty mad then; his face got red 'nd his voice kind uv trembled he wuz so mad.

"Where is its mother?" sez the colonel. "Why is n't she here takin' care uv this hungry 'nd cryin' child like she ought to be?"

"She 's in the front car, sir," sez the young woman, chokin' up. "She 's in the front car in a box, dead; we 're takin' the body 'nd the baby back home."

Now what would you or me have done what would any man have done then 'nd there? Jest what the colonel done.

The colonel did n't wait for no second thought; he jest reached out his big bony hands 'nd he sez, "Young woman, gi' me that baby" sez it so quiet 'nd so gentle like that seemed like it wuz the baby's mother that wuz a speakin'.

The colonel took the baby, and now, may be you won't believe me the colonel held that baby 'nd rocked it in his arms 'nd talked to it like it had been his own child. And the baby seemed to know that it lay ag'in' a lovin' heart, for, when it heerd the ol' man's kind voice 'nd saw his smilin' face 'nd felt the soothin' rockin' uv his arms, the baby stopped its grievin' 'nd cryin', 'nd cuddled up close to the colonel's breast, 'nd begun to coo 'nd laff.

The colonel called the nigger. "Jim," sez he, "you go ahead 'nd tell the conductor to stop the train at the first farm house. We 've got to have some milk for this child some warm milk with sugar into it; I hain't raised a family uv 'leven children for nothin'."

The baby did n't cry no more that night; leastwise we did n't hear it if it did cry. And what if we had heerd it? Blessed if I don't think every last one of us would have got up to help tend that lonesome little thing.

That wuz more 'n twenty years ago, but I kin remember the last words I heerd the colonel say: "No matter if it does cry," sez he. "It don't make no more noise than a cricket, nohow; 'nd I reckon that being a director uv the road I kin stop the train 'nd let off anybody that don't like the way the Han'bul 'nd St. Jo does business."

Twenty years ago! Colonel Elijah Gates is sleepin' in the Palmyry buryin' ground; likely as not the baby has growed up leastwise the Han'bul 'nd St. Jo has; everythink is different now everythink has changed everythink except humin natur', 'nd that is the same, it allus has been, and it allus will be, I reckon.

THE MOTHER IN PARADISE

A mother came to the gateway of Heaven. She was aged and weary. Her body was bowed and her face was wrinkled and withered, for her burden had been the burden of care and trouble and sorrow. So she was glad to be done with life and to seek at the gateway of Heaven the fulfilment of the Promise that had been her solace through all the hard, bitter years.

An angel met the Mother at the gateway, and put her arms about the drooping figure, and spoke gracious, tender words.

"Whom seekest thou?" asked the angel.

"I seek my dear ones who came hither before me," answered the Mother. "They are very many my father, my mother, my husband, my children they all are here together, and for many and weary years I have lived in my loneliness, with no other thing to cheer me but the thought that I should follow them in good time."

"Yes, they are here and they await thee," said the angel. "Lean upon me, dear Mother, and I will lead thee to them."

Then the angel led the way through the garden of Paradise, and the angel and the Mother talked as they walked together.

"I am not weary now," said the Mother, "and my heart is not troubled."

"It is the grace of Heaven that restoreth thee, dear Mother," quoth the angel. "Presently thou shalt be filled with the new life, and thou shalt be young again; and thou shalt sing with rapture, and thy soul shall know the endless ecstasy of Heaven."

"Alas, I care not to be young again," saith the Mother. "I care only to find and to be forever with my beloved ones."

As they journeyed in their way a company came to meet them. Then the Mother saw and knew her dear ones even though the heavenly life had glorified their countenances, the Mother knew them, and she ran to greet them, and there was great joy to her and to them. Meanwhile the angel kept steadfastly at her side.

Now the Mother, when she had embraced her dear ones, looked at each of them separately once more, and then she said: "Ye are indeed my beloved my mother, my father, my husband, and my children! But there is one who should be of your company whom I do not see my babe, my little helpless babe that came hither alone so many, many years ago. My heart fainteth, my breast yearneth for that dear little lamb of mine! Come, let us go together and search for her; or await me here under these pleasant trees while I search and call in this fair garden for my dear, lost little babe!"

The others answered never a word, but the angel said: "I will go with thee, Mother, and together we shall find thy child."

As they went on their way the angel said: "Shall I tell thee of myself? For I was a little helpless babe when I came hither to this fair garden and into this heavenly life."

"Perchance thou knowest her, my precious lambkin!" cried the Mother.

"I was a babe when I came hither," said the angel. "See how I am grown and what happiness hath been mine! The compassion of divinity hath protected and fostered me, and hath led me all these years in the peace that passeth all human understanding. God hath instructed me in wisdom, and He shall instruct thee, too; for all who come hither are as children in His sight, and they shall grow in wisdom and in grace eternally."

"But my babe my own lost little one whom I have not held in these arms for so many weary years shall she not still be my little babe, and shall I not cradle her in my bosom?" asked the Mother.

"Thy child shall be restored to thee," said the angel; "for she yearneth for thee even as thou yearnest for her. Only with this difference, dear Mother: Thy child hath known, in the grace of heavenly wisdom, that at the last thy earthly sorrow should surely be rewarded with the joys of the endless reunion in Paradise!"

"Then she hath thought of me and longed for me to come!" cried the Mother. "And my lost babe shall be restored and shall know her mother again!"

"Ay, she loveth thee fondly," said the angel, "and she hath awaited thy coming, lo, these many years. Presently thine eyes shall be opened and thou shalt see her standing before thee in her heavenly raiment whiter than snow, and around her neck thou shalt see her wearing most precious pearls the tears which thou hast shed, oh lonely Mother! and which are the pearls the little ones in Heaven gather up and cherish as an adornment most pleasing unto God and them."

Then the Mother felt that her eyes were opened, and she turned and looked upon the angel. And the Mother saw that the angel was her lost beloved child whom she was seeking: not the helpless babe that she had thought to find, but a maiden of such heavenly beauty and gentleness as only the dwellers in Paradise behold and know. And the Mother spread her arms, and gave a great cry of joy, and folded her very dear one to her bosom.

Then presently they returned together to the others. And there was rapturous acclaim in Paradise, and it was to God's sweet pleasance that it was so. For a Mother and her beloved communed in the holy companionship of love everlasting.

MR. AND MRS. BLOSSOM

The name we meant to call her was Annette, for that was a name I always liked. 'Way back, before I got married, I made up my mind that if I ever had a daughter I should call her Annette. My intention was good enough, but circumstances of a peculiar nature led me to abandon the idea which in anticipation afforded me really a lot of pleasure. My circumstances have always been humble. I say this in no spirit of complaint. We have very much to be thankful for, and we are particularly grateful for the blessing which heaven has bestowed upon us in the person of our dear child our daughter who comes from school to night to spend Thanksgiving with us and with our friends, Mr. and Mrs. Blossom. I must tell you how we became acquainted with the Blossoms.

When our baby was two years old I used to sit of mornings, before going to my work, on the front steps, watching the baby playing on the sidewalk. This pleasantest half hour of the day I divided between the little one and my pipe. One morning, as I sat there smoking and as the little one was toddling to and fro on the sidewalk, a portly, nice looking old gentleman came down the street, and, as luck would have it, the baby got right in his path, and before I could get to her she tangled herself all up with the old gentleman's legs and cane. The old gentleman seemed very much embarrassed, but, bless your soul! the baby liked it!

"A pretty child a beautiful child!" said the old gentleman, and then he inquired: "Boy or girl?"

"Girl," says I, and I added: "Two years old and weighs thirty pounds."

"That must be a great deal for a little girl to weigh," said the old gentleman, and I saw that his eyes lingered lovingly and yearningly upon the child. I am sure he wanted to say more, but all at once, as if he suddenly recollected himself, he glanced furtively up the street, and then, turning as suddenly the other way, he resumed his course downtown. I thought to myself that he was a kindly old gentleman, a trifle queer, perhaps, but of a gentle nature.

Three or four times within a week after that a similar experience with this old gentleman befell me and the baby. He would greet her cheerily; sometimes he would pat her head, and I saw that his heart warmed toward her. But all the time he talked with us he seemed to act as if he feared he was being watched, and he left us abruptly sometimes breaking away in the middle of a sentence as if he was afraid he might say something he ought not to say. At last, however, I learned that his name was Blossom, and that Mrs. Blossom and he lived alone in a fine house up yonder in a more fashionable part of our street. In an outburst of confidence one morning he told me that he was very fond of children, and that he felt that much was gone out of his life because no little one had ever come to Mary and himself.

"But," he added with an air of assumed cheerfulness, "as Mary does not like children at all, it is perhaps for the best that none has ever come to us."

I now understood why Mr. Blossom was so cautious in his attentions to our baby; he was fearful of being observed by his wife; he felt that it was his duty to humor her in her disinclination to children. I pitied the dear old gentleman, and for the same reason conceived a violent dislike for Mrs. Blossom.

But my wife Cordelia told me something one day that set my heart to aching for both the two old people.

"A sweet looking old lady passed the house this afternoon," said Cordelia, "and took notice of baby asleep in my arms on the porch. She stopped and asked me all about her and presently she kissed her, and then I saw that she was crying softly to herself. I asked her if she had ever lost a little girl, and she said no. 'I have always been childless,' said the sweet old lady. 'In all the years of my wifehood I have besought but one blessing of heaven the joy of maternity. My prayers are unanswered, and it is perhaps better so.' She told me then that her husband did not care for children; she could hardly reconcile his professed antipathy to them with his warm, gentle, and loyal nature; but it was well, if he did not want children, that none had come."

"What was the old lady's name?" I asked.

"Mrs. Blossom," said my wife Cordelia.

I whistled softly to myself. Then I told Cordelia of my experience with Mr. Blossom, and we wondered where and when and how this pathetic comedy of cross purposes would end. We talked the matter over many a time after that, and we agreed that it would be hard to find an instance of deception more touching than that which we had met with in the daily life of Mr. and Mrs. Blossom. Meanwhile the two old people became more and more attached to our precious baby. Every morning brought Mr. Blossom down the street with a smile and a caress and a tender word for the little one, that toddled to meet him and overwhelm him with her innocent prattle. Every afternoon found the sweet looking old lady in front of our house, fondling our child, and feeding her starving maternal instinct upon the little one's caresses. Each one the old gentleman and the old lady each one confessed by action and by word to an overwhelming love for children, yet between them stood that pitiless lie, conceived of the tenderest consideration for each other, but resulting in lifelong misery.

I tell you, it was mighty hard sometimes for Cordelia and me not to break out with the truth!

It occurred to us both that there would eventually come a time when the friendship of Mr. and Mrs. Blossom would be precious indeed to our daughter. We had great hopes of that child, and all our day dreams involved her. She must go to school, she must be educated, she must want nothing; there was no conceivable sacrifice which Cordelia and I would not make gladly for our little girl. Would we be willing to share her love with these two childless old people, who yearned for that love and were ready to repay it with every benefit which riches can supply? We asked ourselves that question a thousand times. God helped us to answer it.

The winter set in early and suddenly. We were awakened one night by that hoarse, terrifying sound which chills the parent heart with anxiety. Our little one was flushed with fever, and there was a rattling in her throat when she breathed. When the doctor came he told us not to be frightened; this was a mild form of croup, he said. His medicines seemed to give relief, for presently the child breathed easier and slept. Next morning an old gentleman on his way downtown wondered why the baby was not out to greet him with a hilarious shout; he felt that here all about his heart which told him that two dimpled hands had taken hold and held him fast. An old lady came to the door that day and asked questions hurriedly and in whispers, and went away crying to herself under her veil.

When it came night again the baby was as good as well. I was rocking her and telling her a story, when the door bell rang. A moment later I could hardly believe my senses, but Mr. Blossom stood before me.

"I heard she was sick," said he, coming up to the cradle and taking the baby's hand awkwardly, but tenderly, in his. "You can never know how I have suffered all day, for this little one has grown very dear to me, and I dare not think what I should do if evil were to befall her. To night I told my wife a lie. I said that I had a business engagement that called me downtown; I told her that in order to hasten here without letting her know the truth. She does not like children; I would not for the world have her know how tenderly I love this little one."

He was still talking to me in this wise when I heard a step upon the stairway. I went to the door and opened it. Mrs. Blossom stood there.

"I have worried all day about the baby," she said, excitedly. "Fortunately, Mr. Blossom was called downtown this evening, and I have run in to ask how our precious baby is. I must go away at once, for he does not care for children, you know, and I would not have him know how dear this babe has grown to me!"

Mrs. Blossom stood on the threshold as she said these words. And then she saw the familiar form of the dear old gentleman bending over the cradle, holding the baby's hands in his. Mr. Blossom had recognized his wife's voice and heard her words.

"Mary!" he cried, and he turned and faced her. She said, "Oh, John!" that was all, and her head drooped upon her breast. So there they stood before each other, confronted by the revelation which they had thought buried in long and many years.

She was the first to speak, for women are braver and stronger than men. She accused herself and took all the blame. But he would not listen to her self reproaches. And they spoke to each other I know not what things, only that they were tender and sweet and of consolation. I remember that at the last he put his arm about her as if he had not been an aged man and she were not white haired and bowed, but as if they two were walking in the springtime of their love.

"It is God's will," he said, "and let us not rebel against it. The journey to the end is but a little longer now; we have come so far together, and surely we can go on alone."

"No, not alone," I said, for the inspiration came to me then. "Our little child yonder God has lent this lambkin to our keeping share her love with us. There is so much, so very much you can do for her which we cannot do, for we are poor, and you are rich. Help us to care for her and share her love with us, and she shall be your child and ours."

That was the compact between us fifteen years ago, and they have been happy, very happy years. Blossom we call her Blossom, after the dear old friends who have been so good to her and to us she comes from school to night, and to morrow we shall sit down to Thanksgiving dinner with our daughter. We always speak of her as "our daughter," for, you know, she belongs now no more to Cordelia and me than to Mr. and Mrs. Blossom.

DEATH AND THE SOLDIER

A soldier, who had won imperishable fame on the battlefields of his country, was confronted by a gaunt stranger, clad all in black and wearing an impenetrable mask.

"Who are you that you dare to block my way?" demanded the soldier.

Then the stranger drew aside his mask, and the soldier knew that he was Death.

"Have you come for me?" asked the soldier. "If so, I will not go with you; so go your way alone."

But Death held out his bony hand and beckoned to the soldier.

"No," cried the soldier, resolutely; "my time is not come. See, here are the histories I am writing no hand but mine can finish them I will not go till they are done!"

"I have ridden by your side day and night," said Death; "I have hovered about you on a hundred battlefields, but no sight of me could chill your heart till now, and now I hold you in my power. Come!"

And with these words Death seized upon the soldier and strove to bear him hence, but the soldier struggled so desperately that he prevailed against Death, and the strange phantom departed alone. Then when he had gone the soldier found upon his throat the imprint of Death's cruel fingers so fierce had been the struggle. And nothing could wash away the marks nay, not all the skill in the world could wash them away, for they were disease, lingering, agonizing, fatal disease. But with quiet valor the soldier returned to his histories, and for many days thereafter he toiled upon them as the last and best work of his noble life.

"How pale and thin the soldier is getting," said the people. "His hair is whitening and his eyes are weary. He should not have undertaken the histories the labor is killing him."

They did not know of his struggle with Death, nor had they seen the marks upon the soldier's throat. But the physicians who came to him, and saw the marks of Death's cruel fingers, shook their heads and said the soldier could not live to complete the work upon which his whole heart was set. And the soldier knew it, too, and many a time he paused in his writing and laid his pen aside and bowed his head upon his hands and strove for consolation in the thought of the great fame he had already won. But there was no consolation in all this. So when Death came a second time he found the soldier weak and trembling and emaciated.

"It would be vain of you to struggle with me now," said Death. "My poison is in your veins, and, see, my dew is on your brow. But you are a brave man, and I will not bear you with me till you have asked one favor, which I will grant."

"Give me an hour to ask the favor," said the soldier. "There are so many things my histories and all give me an hour that I may decide what I shall ask."

And as Death tarried, the soldier communed with himself. Before he closed his eyes forever, what boon should he ask of Death? And the soldier's thoughts sped back over the years, and his whole life came to him like a lightning flash the companionship and smiles of kings, the glories of government and political power, the honors of peace, the joys of conquest, the din of battle, the sweets of a quiet home life upon a western prairie, the gentle devotion of a wife, the clamor of noisy boys, and the face of a little girl ah, there his thoughts lingered and clung.

"Time to complete our work our books our histories," counselled Ambition. "Ask Death for time to do this last and crowning act of our great life."

But the soldier's ears were deaf to the cries of Ambition; they heard another voice the voice of the soldier's heart and the voice whispered: "Nellie Nellie Nellie." That was all no other words but those, and the soldier struggled to his feet and stretched forth his hands and called to Death; and, hearing him calling, Death came and stood before him.

"I have made my choice," said the soldier.

"The books?" asked Death, with a scornful smile.

"No, not them," said the soldier, "but my little girl my Nellie! Give me a lease of life till I have held her in these arms, and then come for me and I will go!"

Then Death's hideous aspect was changed; his stern features relaxed and a look of pity came upon them. And Death said, "It shall be so," and saying this he went his way.

Now the soldier's child was far away many, many leagues from where the soldier lived, beyond a broad, tempestuous ocean. She was not, as you might suppose, a little child, although the soldier spoke of her as such. She was a wife and a mother; yet even in her womanhood she was to the soldier's heart the same little girl the soldier had held upon his knee many and many a time while his rough hands weaved prairie flowers in her soft, fair curls. And the soldier called her Nellie now, just as he did then, when she sat on his knee and prattled of her dolls. This is the way of the human heart.

It having been noised about that the soldier was dying and that Nellie had been sent for across the sea, all the people vied with each other in soothing the last moments of the famous man, for he was beloved by all and all were bound to him by bonds of patriotic gratitude, since he had been so brave a soldier upon the battlefields of his country. But the soldier did not heed their words of sympathy; the voice of fame, which, in the past, had stirred a fever in his blood and fallen most pleasantly upon his ears, awakened no emotion in his bosom now. The soldier thought only of Nellie, and he awaited her coming.

An old comrade came and pressed his hand, and talked of the times when they went to the wars together; and the old comrade told of this battle and of that, and how such a victory was won and such a city taken. But the soldier's ears heard no sound of battle now, and his eyes could see no flash of sabre nor smoke of war.

So the people came and spoke words of veneration and love and hope, and so with quiet fortitude, but with a hungry heart, the soldier waited for Nellie, his little girl.

She came across the broad, tempestuous ocean. The gulls flew far out from land and told the winds, and the winds flew further still and said to the ship: "Speed on, O ship! speed on in thy swift, straight course, for you are bearing a treasure to a father's heart!"

Then the ship leapt forward in her pathway, and the waves were very still, and the winds kept whispering "Speed on, O ship," till at last the ship was come to port and the little girl was clasped in the soldier's arms.

Then for a season the soldier seemed quite himself again, and people said "He will live," and they prayed that he might. But their hopes and prayers were vain. Death's seal was on the soldier, and there was no release.

The last days of the soldier's life were the most beautiful of all but what a mockery of ambition and fame and all the grand, pretentious things of life they were! They were the triumph of a human heart, and what is better or purer or sweeter than that?

No thought of the hundred battlefields upon which his valor had shown conspicuous came to the soldier now nor the echo of his eternal fame nor even yet the murmurs of a sorrowing people. Nellie was by his side, and his hungry, fainting heart fed on her dear love and his soul went back with her to the years long agone.

Away beyond the western horizon upon the prairie stands a little home over which the vines trail. All about it is the tall, waving grass, and over yonder is the swale with a legion of chattering blackbirds perched on its swaying reeds and rushes. Bright wild flowers bloom on every side, the quail whistles on the pasture fence, and from his home in the chimney corner the cricket tries to chirrup an echo to the lonely bird's call. In this little prairie home we see a man holding on his knee a little girl, who is telling him of her play as he smooths her fair curls or strokes her tiny velvet hands; or perhaps she is singing him one of her baby songs, or asking him strange questions of the great wide world that is so new to her; or perhaps he binds the wild flowers she has brought into a little nosegay for her new gingham dress, or but we see it all, and so, too, does the soldier, and so does Nellie, and they hear the blackbird's twitter and the quail's shrill call and the cricket's faint echo, and all about them is the sweet, subtle, holy fragrance of memory.

And so at last, when Death came and the soldier fell asleep forever, Nellie, his little girl, was holding his hands and whispering to him of those days. Hers were the last words he heard, and by the peace that rested on his face when he was dead you might have thought the soldier was dreaming of a time when Nellie prattled on his knee and bade him weave the wild flowers in her curls.

THE 'JININ' FARMS

You see Bill an' I wuz jest like brothers; wuz raised on 'jinin' farms: he wuz his folks' only child, an' I wuz my folks' only one. So, nat'ril like, we growed up together, lovin' an' sympathizin' with each other. What I knowed, I told Bill, an' what Bill knowed, he told me, an' what neither on us knowed why, that warn't wuth knowin'!

If I had n't got over my braggin' days, I 'd allow that, in our time, Bill an' I wuz jest about the sparkin'est beaus in the township; leastwise that's what the girls thought; but, to be honest about it, there wuz only two uv them girls we courted, Bill an' I, he courtin' one an' I t'other. You see we sung in the choir, an' as our good luck would have it we got sot on the sopranner an' the alto, an' bimeby oh, well, after beauin' 'em round a spell a year or so, for that matter we up an' married 'em, an' the old folks gin us the farms, 'jinin' farms, where we boys had lived all our lives. Lizzie, my wife, had always been powerful friendly with Marthy, Bill's wife; them two girls never met up but what they wuz huggin' an' kissin' an' carryin' on, like girls does; for women ain't like men they can't control theirselves an' their feelin's, like the stronger sext does.

I tell you, it wuz happy times for Lizzie an' me and Marthy an' Bill happy times on the 'jinin' farms, with the pastures full uv fat cattle, an' the barns full uv hay an' grain, and the twin cottages full uv love an' contentment! Then when Cyrus come our little boy our first an' only one! why, when he come, I wuz jest so happy an' so grateful that if I had n't been a man I guess I 'd have hollered maybe cried with joy. Wanted to call the little tyke Bill, but Bill would n't hear to nothin' but Cyrus. You see, he 'd bought a cyclopeedy the winter we wuz all marr'ed an' had been readin' in it uv a great foreign warrior named Cyrus that lived a long spell ago.

"Land uv Goshen, Bill!" sez I, "you don't reckon the baby 'll ever be a warrior?"

"Well, I don't know about that," sez Bill. "There 's no tellin'. At any rate, Cyrus Ketcham has an uncommon sound for a name; so Cyrus it must be, an' when he 's seven years old I 'll gin him the finest Morgan colt in the deestrick!"

So we called him Cyrus, an' he grew up lovin' and bein' loved by everybody.

Well, along about two years or, say, eighteen months or so after Cyrus come to us a little girl baby come to Bill an' Marthy, an' of all the cunnin' sweet little things you ever seen that little girl baby was the cunnin'est an' sweetest! Looked jest like one of them foreign crockery figgers you buy in city stores all pink an' white, with big brown eyes here, an' a teeny, weeney mouth there, an' a nose an' ears, you'd have bet they wuz wax they wuz so small an' fragile. Never darst hold her for fear I 'd break her, an' it liked to skeered me to death to see the way Marthy and Lizzie would kind uv toss her round an' trot her so on their knees or pat her so on the back when she wuz collicky like the wimmin folks sez all healthy babies is afore they 're three months old.

"You 're goin' to have the namin' uv her," sez Bill to me.

"Yes," sez Marthy; "we made it up atween us long ago that you should have the namin' uv our baby like we had the namin' uv yourn."

Then, kind uv hectorin' like for I was always a powerful tease I sez: "How would Cleopatry do for a name? or Venis? I have been readin' the cyclopeedy myself, I 'd have you know!"

An' then I laffed one on them provokin' laffs uv mine oh, I tell ye, I was the worst feller for hectorin' folks you ever seen! But I meant it all in fun, for when I suspicioned they did n't like my funnin', I sez: "Bill," sez I, "an' Marthy, there 's only one name I 'd love above all the rest to call your little lambkin, an' that's the dearest name on earth to me the name uv Lizzie, my wife!"

That jest suited 'em to a T, an' always after that she wuz called leetle Lizzie, an' it sot on her, that name did, like it was made for her, an' she for it. We made it up then perhaps more in fun than anything else that when the children growed up, Cyrus an' leetle Lizzie, they should get marr'd together, an' have both the farms an' be happy, an' be a blessin' to us all in our old age. We made it up in fun, perhaps, but down in our hearts it wuz our prayer jest the same, and God heard the prayer an' granted it to be so.

They played together, they lived together; together they tended deestrick school an' went huckleberryin'; there wuz huskin's an' spellin' bees an' choir meetin's an' skatin' an' slidin' down hill oh, the happy times uv youth! an' all those times our boy Cyrus an' their leetle Lizzie went lovin'ly together!

What made me start so what made me ask of Bill one time: "Are we a gettin' old, Bill?" that wuz the Thanksgivin' night when, as we set round the fire in Bill's front room, Cyrus come to us, holdin' leetle Lizzie by the hand, an' they asked us could they get marr'd come next Thanksgivin' time? Why, it seemed only yesterday that they wuz chicks together! God! how swift the years go by when they are happy years!

"Reuben," sez Bill to me, "le's go down' cellar and draw a pitcher uv cider!"

You see that, bein' men, it wuz n't for us to make a show uv ourselves. Marty an' Lizzie just hugged each other an' laughed an' cried they wuz so glad! Then they hugged Cyrus an' leetle Lizzie; and talk and laff? Well, it did beat all how them women folks did talk and laugh, all at one time! Cyrus laffed, too; an' then he said he reckoned he 'd go out an' throw some fodder in to the steers, and Bill an' I well, we went down cellar to draw that pitcher uv cider.

It ain't for me to tell now uv the meller sweetness uv their courtin' time; I could n't do it if I tried. Oh, how we loved 'em both! Yet, once in the early summer time, our boy Cyrus he come to me an' said: "Father, I want you to let me go away for a spell."

"Cyrus, my boy! Go away?"

"Yes, father; President Linkern has called for soldiers; father, you have always taught me to obey the voice of Duty. That voice summons me now."

"God in heaven," I thought, "you have given us this child only to take him from us!"

But then came the second thought: "Steady, Reuben! You are a man; be a man! Steady, Reuben; be a man!"

"Yer mother," sez I, "yer mother it will break her heart!"

"She leaves it all to you, father."

"But the other the other, Cyrus leetle Lizzie ye know!"

"She is content," sez he.

A storm swep' through me like a cyclone. It wuz all Bill's fault; that warrior name had done it all the cyclopeedy with its lies had pizened Bill's mind to put this trouble on me an' mine!

No, no, a thousand times no! These wuz coward feelin's an' they misbecome me; the ache herein this heart uv mine had no business there. The better part uv me called to me an' said: "Pull yourself together, Reuben Ketcham, and be a man!"

Well, after he went away, leetle Lizzie wuz more to us 'n ever before; wuz at our house all the time; called Lizzie "mother"; wuz contented, in her woman's way, willin' to do her part, waitin' an' watchin' an' prayin' for him to come back. They sent him boxes of good things every fortnight, mother an' leetle Lizzie did; there wuz n't a minute uv the day that they wuz n't talkin' or thinkin' uv him.

Well ye see I must tell it my own way he got killed. In the very first battle Cyrus got killed. The rest uv the soldiers turnt to retreat, because there wuz too many for 'em on the other side. But Cyrus stood right up; he wuz the warrior Bill allowed he wuz goin' to be; our boy wuz n't the kind to run. They tell me there wuz bullet holes here, an' here, an' here all over his breast. We always knew our boy wuz a hero!

Ye can thank God ye wuz n't at the 'jinin' farms when the news come that he 'd got killed. The neighbors, they were there, of course, to kind uv hold us up an' comfort us. Bill an' I sot all day in the woodshed, holdin' hands an' lookin' away from each other, so; never said a word; jest sot there, sympathizin' an' holdin' hands. If we 'd been women, Bill an' I would uv cried an' beat our forrids an' hung round each other's neck, like the womenfolks done. Bein' we wuz men, we jest set there in the woodshed, away from all the rest, holdin' hands an' sympathizin'.

From that time on, leetle Lizzie wuz our daughter our very daughter, all that wuz left to us uv our boy. She never shed a tear; crep' like a shadder 'round the house an' up the front walk an' through the garden. Her heart wuz broke. You could see it in the leetle lambkin's eyes an' hear it in her voice. Wanted to tell her sometimes when she kissed me and called me "father" wanted to tell her, "Leetle Lizzie, let me help ye bear yer load. Speak out the sorrer that's in yer broken heart; speak it out, leetle one, an' let me help yer bear yer load!"

But it is n't for a man to have them feelin's leastwise, it is n't for him to tell uv 'em. So I held my peace and made no sign.

She jest drooped, an' pined, an' died. One mornin' in the spring she wuz standin' in the garden, an' all at oncet she threw her arms up, so, an' fell upon her face, an' when they got to her all thet wuz left to us uv leetle Lizzie wuz her lifeless leetle body. I can't tell of what happened next uv the funeral an' all that. I said this wuz in the spring, an' so it wuz all around us; but it wuz cold and winter here.

One day mother sez to me: "Reuben," sez she, softlike, "Marthy an' I is goin' to the buryin' ground for a spell. Don't you reckon it would be a good time for you to step over an' see Bill while we 're gone?"

"Mebbe so, mother," sez I.

It wuz a pretty day. Cuttin' across lots, I thought to myself what I 'd say to Bill to kind uv comfort him. I made it up that I 'd speak about the time when we wuz boys together; uv how we used to slide down the meetin' house hill, an' go huckleberryin'; uv how I jumped into the pond one day an' saved him from bein' drownded; uv the spellin' school, the huskin' bees, the choir meetin's, the sparkin' times; of the swimmin' hole, the crow's nest in the pine tree, the woodchuck's hole in the old pasture lot; uv the sunny summer days an' the snug winter nights when we wuz boys, an' happy! And then

No, no! I could n't go on like that! I 'd break down. A man can't be a man more 'n jest so far!

Why did mother send me over to see Bill? I 'd better stayed to home! I felt myself chokin' up; if I had n't took a chew uv terbacker, I 'd 'ave been cryin', in a minute!

The nearer I got to Bill's, the worst I hated to go in. Standin' on the stoop, I could hear the tall clock tickin' solemnly inside "tick tock, tick tock," jest as plain as if I wuz settin' aside uv it. The door wuz shet, yet I knew jest what Bill wuz doin'; he was settin' in the old red easy chair, lookin' down at the floor like this. Strange, ain't it, how sometimes when you love folks you know jest what they 're doin', without knowin' anything about it!

There warn't no use knockin', but I knocked three times; so. Did n't say a word; only jest knocked three times that a way. Did n't hear no answer nothin' but the tickin' uv the tall clock; an' yet I knew that Bill heered me an' that down in his heart he was sayin' to me to come in. He never said a word, yet I knowed all the time Bill wuz sayin' for me to come in.

I opened the door, keerful like, an' slipped in. Did n't say nothin'; jest opened the door, softly like, an' slipped in. There set Bill jist as I knowed he was settin', lonesome like, sad like; his head hangin' down; he never looked up at me; never said a word knowed I wuz there all the time, but never said a word an' never made a sign.

How changed Bill wuz oh, Bill, how changed ye wuz! There wuz furrers in yer face an' yer hair wuz white as white as as white as mine! Looked small about the body, thin an' hump shouldered.

Jest two ol' men, that's what we wuz; an' we had been boys together!

Well, I stood there a spell, kind uv hesitatin' like, neither uv us sayin' anything, until bimeby Bill he sort of made a sign for me to set down. Did n't speak, did n't lift his eyes from the floor; only made a sign, like this, in a weak, tremblin' way that wuz all. An' I set down, and there we both set, neither uv us sayin' a word, but both settin' there, lovin' each other an' sympathize' as hard as we could, for that is the way with men.

Bimeby, like we 'd kind uv made it up aforehand, we hitched up closer, for when folks is in sorrer an' trouble they like to be closte together. But not a word all the time, an' hitchin' closer an' closer together, why, bimeby we set side by side. So we set a spell longer, lovin' an' sympathizin', as men folks do; thinkin' uv the old times, uv our boyhood; thinkin' uv the happiness uv the past an' uv all the hopes them two children had brought us! The tall clock ticked, an' that wuz all the sound there wuz, excep' when Bill gin a sigh an' I gin a sigh, too to lighten the load, ye know.

Not a word come from either of us: 't wuz all we could do to set there, lovin' each other an' sympathizin'!

All at oncet for we could n't stand it no longer all at oncet we turnt our faces t' other way an' reached out, so, an' groped with our hands, this way, till we found an' held each other fast in a clasp uv tender meanin'.

Then God forgive me if I done a wrong then I wisht I wuz a woman! For, bein' a woman, I could have riz up, an', standin' so, I could have cried: "Come, Bill! come, let me hold you in these arms; come, let us weep together, an' let this broken heart uv mine speak through these tremblin' lips to that broken heart uv yourn, Bill, tellin' ye how much I love ye an' sympathize with ye!"

But no! I wuz not a woman! I wuz a man! an', bein' a man, I must let my heart break; I must hold my peace, an' I must make no sign.

THE ANGEL AND THE FLOWERS

An angel once asked the Father if he might leave heaven for a day and go down to earth to visit the flowers and birds and little children, for you must know that no other earthly things so much please the angels of heaven as do the flowers, the birds, and the little children.

"Yes," said the Father, "you may go down to earth, but be sure to stay no longer than a day; and when you come back to heaven bring me the loveliest flower you can find, that I may transplant it to my garden and love it for its beauty and its fragrance. Cherish it tenderly, that no harm may befall it."

Then the angel went down to the earth, and he came to a beautiful rose bush upon which bloomed a rose lovelier and more fragrant than any of her kind.

"Heyday, sweet rose," said the angel; "how proudly you hold up your fair head for the winds to kiss."

"Ay, that I do," replied the rose, blushing, albeit she enjoyed the flattery. "But I do not care for these idle zephyrs nor for the wanton sunbeams that dance among my leaves all the day long. To night a cavalier will come hither and tear me from this awkward bush with all its thorns, and kiss me with impassioned lips, and bear me to his lady, who, too, will kiss me and wear me on her bosom, next her heart. That, O angel, is the glory of the rose to be a bearer of kisses from lover to lover, and to hear the whispered vows of the cavalier and his lady, to feel the beating of a gentle heart, and to wither on the white bosom of a wooed maiden."

Then the angel came to a lily that arose fair and majestic from its waxen leaves and bowed gracefully to each passing breeze.

"Why are you so pale and sad, dear lily?" asked the angel.

"My love is the north wind," said the lily, "and I look for him and mourn because he does not come. And when he does come, and I would smile under his caresses, he is cold and harsh and cruel to me, and I wither and die for a season, and when I am wooed back to life again by the smiles and tears of heaven, which are the sunlight and the dew, lo! he is gone."

The angel smiled sadly to hear of the trusting, virgin fidelity of the lily.

"Tell me," asked the lily, "will the north wind come to day?"

"No," said the angel, "nor for many days yet, since it is early summer now."

But the lonely lily did not believe the angel's words. Still looking for her cruel lover, she held her pale face aloft and questioned each zephyr that hurried by. And the angel went his way.

And the angel came next to a daisy that thrived in a meadow where the cattle were grazing and the lambs were frisking.

"Nay, do not pluck me, sir," cried the daisy, merrily; "I would not exchange my home in this smiling pasture for a place upon the princess' bosom."

"You seem very blithesome, little daisy," quoth the angel.

"So I am, and why should I not be?" rejoined the daisy. "The dews bathe me with their kisses, and the stars wink merrily at me all the night through, and during the day the bees come and sing their songs to me, and the little lambs frisk about me, and the big cattle caress me gently with their rough tongues, and all seem to say 'Bloom on, little daisy, for we love you.' So we frolic here on the meadow all the time the lambs, the bees, the cattle, the stars, and I and we are very, very happy."

Next the angel came to a camellia which was most beautiful to look upon. But the camellia made no reply to the angel's salutation, for the camellia, having no fragrance, is dumb for flowers, you must know, speak by means of their scented breath. The camellia, therefore, could say no word to the angel, so the angel walked on in silent sadness.

"Look at me, good angel," cried the honeysuckle; "see how adventuresome I am. At the top of this trellis dwells a ladybird, and in her cozy nest are three daughters, the youngest of whom I go to woo. I carry sweetmeats with me to tempt the pretty dear; do you think she will love me?"

The angel laughed at the honeysuckle's quaint conceit, but made no reply, for yonder he saw a purple aster he fain would question.

"Are you then so busy," asked the angel, "that you turn your head away from every other thing and look always into the sky?"

"Do not interrupt me," murmured the purple aster. "I love the great luminous sun, and whither he rolls in the blazing heavens I turn my face in awe and veneration. I would be the bride of the sun, but he only smiles down upon my devotion and beauty!"

So the angel wandered among the flowers all the day long and talked with them. And toward evening he came to a little grave which was freshly made.

"Do not tread upon us," said the violets. "Let us cluster here over this sacred mound and sing our lullabies."

"To whom do you sing, little flowers?" asked the angel.

"We sing to the child that lies sleeping beneath us," replied the violets. "All through the seasons, even under the snows of winter, we nestle close to this mound and sing to the sleeping child. None but he hears us, and his soul is lulled by our gentle music."

"But do you not often long for other occupation, for loftier service?" inquired the angel.

"Nay," said the violets, "we are content, for we love to sing to the little, sleeping child."

The angel was touched by the sweet humility of these modest flowers. He wept, and his tears fell upon the grave, and the flowers drank up the angel tears and sang more sweetly than before, but so softly that only the sleeping child heard them.

And when the angel flew back to heaven, he cherished a violet in his bosom.

THE CHILD'S LETTER

Everybody was afraid of the old governor because he was so cross and surly. And one morning he was crosser and surlier than ever, because he had been troubled for several days with a matter which he had already decided, but which many people wished to have reversed. A man, found guilty of a crime, had been imprisoned, and there were those who, convinced of his penitence and knowing that his family needed his support, earnestly sought his pardon. To all these solicitations the old governor replied "no," and, having made up his mind, the old governor had no patience with those who persisted in their intercessions. So the old governor was in high dudgeon one morning, and when he came to his office he said to his secretary: "Admit no one to see me; I am weary of these constant and senseless importunities."

Now, the secretary had a discreet regard for the old governor's feelings, and it was seldom that his presence of mind so far deserted him as to admit of his suffering the old governor's wishes to be disregarded. He bolted the door and sat himself down at his modest desk and simulated intense enthusiasm in his work. His simulation was more intense than usual, for never before had the secretary seen the old governor in such a harsh mood.

"Has the mail come where are the papers and the letters?" demanded the old governor, in a gruff voice.

"Here they are, sir," said the secretary, as he put the bundle on the old governor's table. "These are addressed to you privately; the business letters are on my desk. Would you like to see them now?"

"No, not now," growled the old governor; "I will read the papers and my private correspondence first."

But the old governor found cause for uneasiness in this employment. The papers discussed the affair of the imprisoned man, and these private letters came from certain of the old governor's friends, who, strangely enough, exhibited an interest in the self same prisoner's affair. The old governor was highly disgusted.

"They should mind their own business," muttered the old governor. "The papers are very officious, and these other people are simply impertinent. My mind is made up nothing shall change me!"

Then the old governor turned to his private secretary and bade him bring the business letters, and presently the private secretary could hear the old governor growling and fumbling over the pile of correspondence. He knew why the old governor was so excited; many of these letters were petitions from the people touching the affair of the imprisoned man. Oh, how they angered the old governor!

"Humph!" said the old governor at last, "I 'm glad I 'm done with them. There are no more, I suppose."

When the secretary made no reply the old governor was surprised. He wheeled in his chair and searchingly regarded the secretary over his spectacles. He saw that the secretary was strangely embarrassed.

"You have not shown me all," said the old governor, sternly. "What is it you have kept back?"

Then the secretary said: "I had thought not to show it to you. It is nothing but a little child's letter I thought I should not bother you with it."

The old governor was interested. A child's letter to him what could it be about? Such a thing had never happened to him before.

"A child's letter; let me see it," said the old governor, and, although his voice was harsh, somewhat of a tender light came into his eyes.

"'T is nothing but a scrawl," explained the secretary, "and it comes from the prisoner's child Monckton's little girl Monckton, the forger, you know. Of course there's nothing to it a mere scrawl; for the child is only four years old. But the gentleman who sends it says the child brought it to him and asked him to send it to the governor, and then, perhaps, the governor would send her papa home."

The old governor took the letter, and he scanned it curiously. What a wonderful letter it was, and who but a little child could have written it! Such strange hieroglyphics and such crooked lines oh! it was a wonderful letter, as you can imagine.

But the old governor saw something more than the strange hieroglyphics and crooked lines and rude pencillings. He could see in and between the lines of the little child's letter a sweetness and a pathos he had never seen before, and on the crumpled sheet he found a love like the love his bereaved heart had vainly yearned for, oh! so many years.

He saw, or seemed to see, a little head bending over the crumpled page, a dimpled hand toiling at its rude labor of love, and an earnest little face smiling at the thought that this labor would not be in vain. And how wearied the little hand grew and how sleepy the little head became, but the loyal little heart throbbed on and on with patient joy, and neither hand nor head rested till the task was done.

Sweet innocence of childhood! Who would molest thee who bring thee one shadow of sorrow? Who would not rather brave all dangers, endure all fatigues, and bear all burdens to shield thee from the worldly ills thou dream'st not of!

So thought the old governor, as he looked upon the crumpled page and saw and heard the pleadings of the child's letter; for you must know that from the crumpled page there stole a thousand gentle voices that murmured in his ears so sweetly that his heart seemed full of tears. And the old governor thought of his own little one God rest her innocent soul. And it seemed to him as if he could hear her dear baby voice joining with this other's in trustful pleading.

The secretary was amazed when the old governor said to him: "Give me a pardon blank." But what most amazed the secretary was the tremulous tenderness in the old governor's voice and the mistiness behind the old governor's spectacles as he folded the crumpled page reverently and put it carefully in the breast pocket of his greatcoat.

"Humph," thought the secretary, "the old governor has a kinder heart than any of us suspected."

Then, when the prisoner was pardoned and came from his cell, people grasped him by the hand and said: "Our eloquence and perseverance saved you. The old governor could not withstand the pressure we brought to bear on him!"

But the secretary knew, and the old governor, too God bless him for his human heart! They knew that it was the sacred influence of a little child's letter that had done it all that a dimpled baby hand had opened those prison doors.

Once, as Death walked the earth in search of some fair flower upon which he could breathe his icy breath, he met the graceful and pleasing spirit who is called Ambition.

"Good morrow," quoth Death, "let us journey a time together. Both of us are hale fellows; let us henceforth be travelling companions."

Now Ambition is one of the most easily cajoled persons in the world. The soft words of Death flattered him. So Death and Ambition set out together, hand in hand.

And having come into a great city, they were walking in a fine street when they beheld at the window of a certain house a lady who was named Griselda. She was sitting at the window, fondling in her lap her child, a beautiful little infant that held out his dimpled arms to the mother and prattled sweet little things which only a mother can understand.

"What a beautiful lady," said Ambition, "and what a wonderful song she is singing to the child."

"You may praise the mother as you will," said Death, "but it is the child which engages my attention and absorbs my admiration. How I wish the child were mine!"

But Ambition continued to regard Griselda with an eye of covetousness; the song Griselda sang to her babe seemed to have exerted a wondrous spell over the spirit.

"I know a way," suggested Death, "by which we can possess ourselves of these two you of the mother and I of the child."

Ambition's eyes sparkled. He longed for the beautiful mother.

"Tell me how I may win her," said he to Death, "and you shall have the babe."

So Death and Ambition walked in the street and talked of Griselda and her child.

Griselda was a famous singer. She sang in the theatre of the great city, and people came from all parts of the world to hear her songs and join in her praise. Such a voice had never before been heard, and Griselda's fame was equalled only by the riches which her art had brought her. In the height of her career the little babe came to make her life all the sweeter, and Griselda was indeed very happy.

"Who is that at the door?" inquired Charlotte, the old nurse. "It must be somebody of consequence, for he knocks with a certain confidence only those in authority have."

"Go to the door and see," said Griselda.

So Charlotte went to the door, and lo, there was a messenger from the king, and the messenger was accompanied by two persons attired in royal robes.

These companions were Ambition and Death, but they were so splendidly arrayed you never would have recognized them.

"Does the Lady Griselda abide here?" asked the messenger.

"She does," replied old Charlotte, courtesying very low, for the brilliant attire of the strangers dazzled her.

"I have a message from the king," said the messenger.

Old Charlotte could hardly believe her ears. A message from the king! Never before had such an honor befallen one in Griselda's station.

The message besought Griselda to appear in the theatre that night before the king, who knew of her wondrous voice, but had never heard it. And with the message came a royal gift of costly jewels, the like of which Griselda had never set eyes upon.

"You cannot refuse," said Ambition in a seductive voice. "Such an opportunity never before was accorded you and may never again be offered. It is the king for whom you are to sing!"

Griselda hesitated and cast a lingering look at her babe.

"Have no fear for the child," said Death, "for I will care for him while you are gone."

So, between the insinuating advice of Ambition and the fair promises of Death, Griselda was persuaded, and the messenger bore back to the king word that Griselda would sing for him that night.

But Ambition and Death remained as guests in Griselda's household.

The child grew restless as the day advanced. From the very moment that Death had entered the house the little one had seemed very changed, but Griselda was so busy listening to the flattering speeches of Ambition that she did not notice the flush on her infant's cheeks and the feverish rapidity of his breathing.

But Death sat grimly in a corner of the room and never took his eyes from the crib where the little one lay.

"You shall so please the king with your beautiful face and voice," said Ambition, "that he will confer wealth and title upon you. You will be the most famous woman on earth; better than that, your fame shall live always in history it shall be eternal!"

And Griselda smiled, for the picture was most pleasing.

"The child's hands are hot," said old Charlotte, the nurse, "and there seem to be strange tremors in his little body, and he groans as he tosses from one side of his cradle to the other."

Griselda was momentarily alarmed, but Ambition only laughed.

"Nonsense," quoth Ambition, "'tis an old woman's fancy. This envious old witch would have you disappoint the king the king, who would load you with riches and honors!"

So the day lengthened, and Griselda listened to the grateful flatteries of Ambition. But Death sat all the time gazing steadfastly on the little one in the cradle. The candles were brought, and Griselda arrayed herself in her costliest robes.

"I must look my best," she said, "for this is to be the greatest triumph of my life."

"You are very beautiful; you will captivate the king," said Ambition.

"The child is very ill," croaked old Charlotte, the nurse; "he does not seem to be awake nor yet asleep, and there is a strange, hoarse rattling in his breathing."

"For shame!" cried Ambition. "See how the glow of health mantles his cheeks and how the fire of health burns in his eyes."

And Griselda believed the words of Ambition. She did not stoop to kiss her little one. She called his name and threw him a kiss, and hastened to her carriage in the street below. The child heard the mother's voice, raised his head, and stretched forth his hands to Griselda, but she was gone and Ambition had gone with her. But Death remained with Griselda's little one.

The theatre was more brilliant that night than ever before. It had been noised about that Griselda would sing for the king, and lords and ladies in their most imposing raiment filled the great edifice to overflowing, while in the royal box sat the king himself, with the queen and the princes and the princesses.

"It will be a great triumph," said Ambition to Griselda, and Griselda knew that she had never looked half so beautiful nor felt half so ready for the great task she had to perform. There was mighty cheering when she swept before the vast throng, and the king smiled and bowed when he saw that Griselda wore about her neck the costly jewels he had sent her. But if the applause was mighty when she appeared, what was it when she finished her marvellous song and bowed herself from the stage! Thrice was she compelled to repeat the song, and a score of times was she recalled to receive the homage of the delighted throng. Bouquets of beautiful flowers were heaped about her feet, and with his own hand from his box the king threw to her a jewelled necklace far costlier than his previous gift.

As Griselda hurried from her dressing room to her carriage she marvelled that Ambition had suddenly and mysteriously quitted her presence. In his place stood the figure of a woman, all in black, and with large, sad eyes and pale face.

"Who are you?" asked Griselda.

"I am the Spirit of Eternal Sorrow," said the woman.

And the strange, sad woman went with Griselda into the carriage and to Griselda's home.

Old Charlotte, the nurse, met them at the door. She was very white and she trembled as if with fear.

Then Griselda seemed to awaken from a dream.

"My child?" she asked, excitedly.

"He is gone," replied old Charlotte, the nurse.

Griselda flew to the chamber where she had left him. There stood the little cradle where he had lain, but the cradle was empty.

"Who has taken him away?" cried Griselda, sinking upon her knees and stretching her hands in agony to heaven.

"Death took him away but an hour ago," said old Charlotte, the nurse.

Then Griselda thought of his fevered face and his pitiful little moans and sighs; of the guileful flatteries of Ambition that had deafened her mother ears to the pleadings of her sick babe; of the brilliant theatre and the applause of royalty and of the last moments of her lonely, dying child.

And Griselda arose and tore the jewels from her breast and threw them far from her and cried: "O God, it is my punishment! I am alone."

"Nay, not so, O mother," said a solemn voice; "I am with thee and will abide with thee forever."

Griselda turned and looked upon the tall, gloomy figure that approached her with these words.

It was the Spirit of Eternal Sorrow.

THE TWO WIVES

In a certain city there were two wives named Gerda and Hulda. Although their homes adjoined, these wives were in very different social stations, for Gerda was the wife of a very proud and very rich man, while Hulda was the wife of a humble artisan. Gerda's house was lofty and spacious and was adorned with most costly and most beautiful things, but Hulda's house was a scantily furnished little cottage. The difference in their social stations did not, however, prevent Gerda and Hulda from being very friendly in a proper fashion, and the two frequently exchanged visits while their husbands were away from home.

One day Hulda was at Gerda's house, and Gerda said: "I must show you the painting we have just received from Paris. It is the most beautiful painting in the world, and it cost a princely sum of money."

And Gerda took Hulda into an adjoining chamber and uncovered the picture, and for a long time Hulda stood admiring it in silence. It was indeed a masterpiece of art. Such beauty of conception, such elegance of design, and such nicety in execution had never before been seen. It was a marvel of figure and color and effect.

"Is it not the most beautiful picture in all the world?" asked Gerda.

"It is very beautiful," replied Hulda, "but it is not the most beautiful picture in all the world."

Then Gerda took Hulda into another chamber and showed her a jewelled music box which the most cunning artisans in all Switzerland had labored for years to produce.

"You shall hear it make music," said Gerda.

And Gerda touched the spring, and the music box discoursed a harmony such as Hulda's listening ears had never heard before. It seemed as if a mountain brook, a summer zephyr, and a wild wood bird were in the box vying with each other in sweet melodies.

"Is it not the most beautiful music in all the world?" asked Gerda.

"It is very beautiful," replied Hulda, "but it is not the most beautiful music in all the world."

Then Gerda was sorely vexed.

"You said that of the picture," said Gerda, "and you say it of the music. Now tell me, Hulda, where is there to be found a more beautiful picture, and where more beautiful music?"

"Come with me, Gerda," said Hulda.

And Hulda led Gerda from the stately mansion into her own humble little cottage.

"See there upon the wall near the door?" said Hulda.

"I see nothing but stains and marks of dirt," said Gerda. "Where is the picture of which you spoke?"

"They are the prints of a baby hand," said Hulda. "You are a woman and a wife, and would you not exchange all the treasures of your palace for the finger marks of a little hand upon your tinted walls?"

And Gerda made no reply.

Then Hulda went to a corner and drew forth a pair of quaint, tiny shoes and showed them to Gerda.

"These are a baby's shoes," said Hulda, "and make a music no art can equal. Other sounds may charm the ear and delight the senses, but the music of a baby's shoe thrills the heart and brings the soul into communion with the angels."

Then Gerda cried "'T is true, O Hulda! 't is true." And she bowed her head and wept. For she was childless.

THE WOOING OF MISS WOPPIT

At that time the camp was new. Most of what was called the valuable property was owned by an English syndicate, but there were many who had small claims scattered here and there on the mountainside, and Three fingered Hoover and I were rightly reckoned among these others. The camp was new and rough to the degree of uncouthness, yet, upon the whole, the little population was well disposed and orderly. But along in the spring of '81, finding that we numbered eight hundred, with electric lights, telephones, a bank, a meeting house, a race track, and such like modern improvements, we of Red Hoss Mountain became possessed of the notion to have a city government; so nothing else would do but to proceed at once and solemnly to the choice of a mayor, marshal, clerk, and other municipal officers. The spirit of party politics (as it is known and as it controls things elsewhere) did not enter into the short and active canvass; there were numerous candidates for each office, all were friends, and the most popular of the lot were to win. The campaign was fervent but good natured.

I shall venture to say that Jim Woppit would never have been elected city marshal but for the potent circumstance that several of the most influential gentlemen in the camp were in love with Jim's sister; that was Jim's hold on these influences, and that was why he was elected.

Yet Jim was what you 'd call a good fellow not that he was fair to look upon, for he was not; he was swarthy and heavy featured and hulking; but he was a fair speaking man, and he was always ready to help out the boys when they went broke or were elsewise in trouble. Yes, take him all in all, Jim Woppit was properly fairly popular, although, as I shall always maintain, he would never have been elected city marshal over Buckskin and Red Drake and Salty Boardman if it had n't been (as I have intimated) for the backing he got from Hoover, Jake Dodsley, and Barber Sam. These three men last named were influences in the camp, enterprising and respected citizens, with plenty of sand in their craws and plenty of stuff in their pockets; they loved Miss Woppit, and they were in honor bound to stand by the interests of the brother of that fascinating young woman.

I was not surprised that they were smitten; she might have caught me, too, had it not been for the little woman and the three kids back in the states. As handsome and as gentle a lady was Miss Woppit as ever walked a white pine floor so very different from White River Ann, and Red Drake's wife, and old man Edgar's daughter, for they were magpies who chattered continually and maliciously, hating Miss Woppit because she wisely chose to have nothing to do with them. She lived with her brother Jim on the side hill, just off the main road, in the cabin that Smooth Ephe Hicks built before he was thrown off his broncho into the gulch. It was a pretty but lonesome place, about three quarters of a mile from the camp, adjoining the claim which Jim Woppit worked in a lazy sort of way Jim being fairly well fixed, having sold off a coal farm in Illinois just before he came west.

In this little cabin abode Miss Woppit during the period of her wooing, a period covering, as I now recall, six or, may be, eight months. She was so pretty, so modest, so diligent, so homekeeping, and so shy, what wonder that those lonely, heart hungry men should fall in love with her? In all the population of the camp the number of women was fewer than two score, and of this number half were married, others were hopeless spinsters, and others were irretrievably bad, only excepting Miss Woppit, the prettiest, the tidiest, the gentlest of all. She was good, pure, and lovely in her womanliness; I shall not say that I envied no, I respected Hoover and Dodsley and Barber Sam for being stuck on the girl; you 'd have respected 'em, too, if you 'd seen her and and them. But I did take it to heart because Miss Woppit seemed disinclined to favor any suit for her fair hand particularly because she was by no means partial to Three fingered Hoover, as square a man as ever struck pay dirt dear old pardner, your honest eyes will never read these lines, between which speaks my lasting love for you!

In the first place, Miss Woppit would never let the boys call on her of an evening unless her brother Jim was home; she had strict notions about that sort of thing which she would n't waive. I reckon she was right according to the way society looks at these things, but it was powerful hard on Three fingered Hoover and Jake Dodsley and Barber Sam to be handicapped by etiquette when they had their bosoms chock full of love and were dying to tell the girl all about it.

Jake Dodsley came a heap nearer than the others to letting Miss Woppit know what his exact feelings were. He was a poet of no mean order. What he wrote was printed regularly in Cad Davis' Leadville paper under the head of "Pearls of Pegasus," and all us Red Hoss Mountain folks allowed that next to Willie Pabor of Denver our own Jake Dodsley had more of the afflatus in him than any other living human poet. Hoover appreciated Jake's genius, even though Jake was his rival. It was

Jake's custom to write poems at Miss Woppit poems breathing the most fervid sentiment, all about love and bleeding hearts and unrequited affection. The papers containing these effusions he would gather together with rare diligence, and would send them, marked duly with a blue or a red pencil, to Miss Woppit.

The poem which Hoover liked best was one entitled "True Love," and Hoover committed it to memory yes, he went even further; he hired Professor De Blanc (Casey's piano player) to set it to music, and this office the professor discharged nobly, producing a simple but solemn like melody which Hoover was wont to sing in feeling wise, poor, dear, misguided fellow that he was! Seems to me I can hear his big, honest, husky, voice lifted up even now in rendition of that expression of his passion:

Turrue love never dies
Like a river flowin'
In its course it gathers force,
Broader, deeper growin';
Strength'nin' in the storms 'at come,
Triumphin' in sorrer,
Till To day fades away
In the las' To morrer.
Wot though Time flies?
Turrue love never dies!

Moreover, Three fingered Hoover discoursed deftly upon the fiddle; at obligates and things he was not much, but at real music he could not be beat. Called his fiddle "Mother," because his own mother was dead, and being he loved her and had no other way of showing it, why, he named his fiddle after her. Three fingered Hoover was full of just such queer conceits.

Barber Sam was another music genius; his skill as a performer upon the guitar was one of the marvels of the camp. Nor had he an indifferent voice Prof. De Blanc allowed that if Barber Sam's voice had been cultured at the proper time by which I suppose he meant in youth Barber Sam would undoubtedly have become "one of the brightest constellations in the operatic firmament." Moreover, Barber Sam had a winsome presence; a dapper body was he, with a clear olive skin, soulful eyes, a noble mustache, and a splendid suit of black curly hair. His powers of conversation were remarkable that fact, coupled with his playing the guitar and wearing plaid clothes, gave him the name of Barber Sam, for he was not really a barber; was only just like one.

In the face of all their wooing, Miss Woppit hardened her heart against these three gentlemen, any one of whom the highest lady in the land might have been proud to catch. The girl was not inclined to affairs of the heart; she cared for no man but her brother Jim. What seemed to suit her best was to tend to things about the cabin it was called The Bower, the poet Jake Dodsley having given it that name to till the little garden where the hollyhocks grew, and to stroll away by herself on the hillside or down through Magpie Glen, beside the gulch. A queer, moodful creature she was; unlike other girls, so far as we were able to judge. She just doted on Jim, and Jim only how she loved that brother you shall know presently.

It was lucky that we organized a city government when we did. All communities have streaks of bad luck, and it was just after we had elected a mayor, a marshal, and a full quota of officers that Red Hoss Mountain had a spell of experiences that seemed likely at one time to break up the camp. There 's no telling where it all would have ended if we had n't happened to have a corps of vigilant and brave men in office, determined to maintain law and order at all personal hazards. With a camp, same as 'tis with dogs, it is mighty unhealthy to get a bad name.

The tidal wave of crime if I may so term it struck us three days after the election. I remember distinctly that all our crowd was in at Casey's, soon after nightfall, indulging in harmless pleasantries, such as eating, drinking, and stud poker. Casey was telling how he had turned several cute tricks on election day, and his recital recalled to others certain exciting experiences they had had in the states; so, in an atmosphere of tobacco, beer, onions, wine, and braggadocio, and with the further delectable stimulus of seven year old McBrayer, the evening opened up congenially and gave great promise. The boys were convivial, if not boisterous. But Jim Woppit, wearing the big silver star of his exalted office on his coat front, was present in the interests of peace and order, and the severest respect was shown to the newly elected representative of municipal dignity and authority.

All of a sudden, sharp, exacting, and staccato like, the telephone sounded; seemed like it said, "Quick trouble help!" By the merest chance a lucky chance Jim Woppit happened to be close by, and he reached for the telephone and answered the summons.

"Yes." "Where?" "You bet right away!"

That was what Jim said; of course, we heard only one side of the talk. But we knew that something something remarkable had happened. Jim was visibly excited; he let go the telephone, and, turning around, full over against us, he said, "By—, boys! the stage hez been robbed!"

A robbery! The first in the Red Hoss Mountain country! Every man leapt to his feet and broke for the door, his right hand thrust instinctively back toward his hip pocket. There was blood in every eye.

Hank Eaves' broncho was tied in front of Casey's.

"Tell me where to go," says Hank, "and I 'll git thar in a minnit. I 'm fixed."

"No, Hank," says Jim Woppit, commanding like, "I 'll go. I 'm city marshal, an' it's my place to go I 'm the repersentive of law an' order an' I 'll enforce 'em damn me ef I don't!"

"That's bizness Jim's head 's level!" cried Barber Sam.

"Let Jim have the broncho," the rest of us counselled, and Hank had to give in, though he hated to, for he was spoiling for trouble cussedest fellow for fighting you ever saw! Jim threw himself astride the spunky little broncho and was off like a flash.

"Come on, boys," he called back to us; "come on, ez fast ez you kin to the glen!"

Of course we could n't anywhere near keep up with him; he was soon out of sight. But Magpie Glen was only a bit away just a trifle up along the main road beyond the Woppit cabin. Encouraged by the excitement of the moment and by the whooping of Jake Dodsley, who opined (for being a poet he always opined) that some evil might have befallen his cherished Miss Woppit incited by these influences we made all haste. But Miss Woppit was presumably safe, for as we hustled by The Bower we saw the front room lighted up and the shadow of Miss Woppit's slender figure flitting to and fro behind the white curtain. She was frightened almost to death, poor girl!

It appeared from the story of Steve Barclay, the stage driver, that along about eight o'clock the stage reached the glen a darkish, dismal spot, and the horses, tired and sweaty, toiled almost painfully up the short stretch of rising ground. There were seven people in the stage: Mr. Mills, superintendent of the Royal Victoria mine; a travelling man (or drummer) from Chicago, one Pryor, an invalid tenderfoot, and four miners returning from a round up at Denver. Steve Barclay was the only person outside. As the stage reached the summit of the little hill the figure of a man stole suddenly from the thicket by the roadside, stood directly in front of the leading horses, and commanded a halt. The movement was so sudden as to terrify the horses, and the consequence was that, in shying, the brutes came near tipping the coach completely over. Barclay was powerless to act, for the assailant covered him with two murderous revolvers and bade him throw up his hands.

Then the men in the coach were ordered out and compelled to disgorge their valuables, the robber seeming to identify and to pay particular attention to Mr. Mills, the superintendent, who had brought with him from Denver a large sum of money. When the miners made a slight show of resistance the assailant called to his comrades in the bush to fire upon the first man who showed fight; this threat induced a wise resignation to the inevitable. Having possessed himself in an incredibly short time of his booty, the highwayman backed into the thicket and quickly made off. The procedure from first to last occupied hardly more than five minutes.

The victims of this outrage agreed that the narrative as I have given it was in the main correct. Barclay testified that he saw the barrels of rifles gleaming from the thicket when the outlaw called to his confederates. On the other hand, Mr. Mills, who was the principal loser by the affair, insisted that the outlaw did his work alone, and that his command to his alleged accomplices was merely a bluff. There was, too, a difference in the description given of the highwayman, some of the party describing him as a short, thick set man, others asserting that he was tall and slender. Of his face no sight had been obtained, for he wore a half mask and a large slouch hat pulled well down over his ears. But whatever dispute there may have been as to details, one thing was sure robbery had been done, and the robber had fled with four gold watches and cash to the amount of, say, two thousand five hundred dollars.

Recovering betimes from their alarm and bethinking themselves of pursuit of the outlaws, the helpless victims proceeded to push into camp to arouse the miners. It was then that Barclay discovered that the tire of one of the front wheels had come off in the jolt and wrench caused by the frightened horses. As no time was to be lost, Barclay suggested that somebody run down the road to Woppit's cabin and telephone to camp. Mr. Mills and the Chicago drummer undertook this errand. After considerable parley for Miss Woppit wisely insisted upon being convinced of her visitors' honorable intentions these two men were admitted, and so the alarm was transmitted to Casey's, Miss Woppit meanwhile exhibiting violent alarm lest her brother Jim should come to harm in pursuing the fugitives.

As for Jim Woppit, he never once lost his head. When the rest of us came up to the scene of the robbery he had formed a plan of pursuit. It was safe, he said, to take for granted that there was a gang of the outlaws. They would undoubtedly strike for Eagle Pass, since there was no possible way of escape in the opposite direction, the gulch, deep and wide, following the main road close into camp. Ten of us should go with him ten of the huskiest miners mounted upon the stanchest bronchoes the camp could supply. "We shall come up with the hellions before mornin'," said he, and then he gritted his teeth significantly. A brave man and a cool man, you 'll allow; good hearted, too, for in the midst of all the excitement he thought of his sister, and he said, almost tenderly, to Three fingered Hoover: "I can trust you, pardner, I know. Go up to the cabin and tell her it's all right that I 'll be back to morrow and that she must n't be skeered. And if she is skeered, why, you kind o' hang round there to night and act like you knew everything was all O. K."

"But may be Hoover 'll be lonesome," suggested Barber Sam. He was a sly dog.

"Then you go 'long too," said Jim Woppit. "Tell her I said so."

Three fingered Hoover would rather a good deal rather have gone alone. Yet, with all that pardonable selfishness, he recognized a certain impropriety in calling alone at night upon an unprotected female. So Hoover accepted, though not gayly, of Barber Sam's escort, and in a happy moment it occurred to the twain that it might be a pious idea to take their music instruments with them. Hardly, therefore, had Jim Woppit and his posse flourished out of camp when Three fingered Hoover and Barber Sam, carrying Mother and the famous guitar, returned along the main road toward The Bower.

When the cabin came in view the cabin on the side hill with hollyhocks standing guard round it one of those subtle fancies in which Barber Sam's active brain abounded possessed Barber Sam. It was to convey to Miss Woppit's ear good tidings upon the wings of music. "Suppose we play 'All's Well'?" suggested Barber Sam. "That'll let her know that everything's O. K."

"Just the thing!" answered Three fingered Hoover, and then he added, and he meant it: "Durned if you ain't jest about as slick as they make 'em, pardner!"

The combined efforts of the guitar and Mother failed, however, to produce any manifestation whatever, so far as Miss Woppit was concerned. The light in the front room of the cabin glowed steadily, but no shadow of the girl's slender form was to be seen upon the white muslin curtain. So the two men went up the gravelly walk and knocked firmly but respectfully at the door.

They had surmised that Miss Woppit might be asleep, but, oh, no, not she. She was not the kind of sister to be sleeping when her brother was in possible danger. The answer to the firm but respectful knocking was immediate.

"Who's there and what do you want?" asked Miss Woppit in tremulous tones, with her face close to the latch. There was no mistaking the poor thing's alarm.

"It's only us gents," answered Three fingered Hoover, "me an' Barber Sam; did n't you hear us serenadin' you a minnit ago? We 've come to tell you that everything 's all right Jim told us to come he told us to tell you not to be skeered, and if you wuz skeered how we gents should kind of hang round here to night; be you skeered, Miss Woppit? Your voice sounds sort o' like you wuz."

Having now unbolted and unlatched and opened the door, Miss Woppit confessed that she was indeed alarmed; the pallor of her face confirmed that confession. Where was Jim? Had they caught the robbers? Was there actually no possibility of Jim's getting shot or stabbed or hurt? These and similar questions did the girl put to the two men, who, true to their trust, assured the timorous creature in well assumed tones of confidence that her brother could n't get hurt, no matter how hard he might try.

To make short of a long tale, I will say that the result of the long parley, in which Miss Woppit exhibited a most charming maidenly embarrassment, was that Three fingered Hoover and Barber Sam were admitted to the cabin for the night. It was understood nay, it was explicitly set forth, that they should have possession of the front room wherein they now stood, while Miss Woppit was to retire to her apartment beyond, which, according to popular fame and in very truth, served both as a kitchen and Miss Woppit's bedroom, there being only two rooms in the cabin.

This front room had in it a round table, a half dozen chairs, a small sheet iron stove, and a rude kind of settee that served Jim Woppit for a bed by night. There were some pictures hung about on the walls neither better nor poorer than the pictures invariably found in the homes of miners. There was the inevitable portrait of John C. Fremont and the inevitable print of the pathfinder planting his flag on the summit of Pike's Peak; a map of Colorado had been ingeniously invested with an old looking glass frame, and there were several cheap chromos of flowers and fruit, presumably Miss Woppit's contributions to the art stores of the household. Upon the centre table, which was covered with a square green cloth, stood a large oil lamp, whose redolence and constant spluttering testified pathetically to its neglect. There were two books on the table viz., an old "Life of Kit Carson" and a bound file of the "Police News," abounding, as you will surmise, in atrocious delineations of criminal life. We can understand that a volume of police literature would not be out of place in the home of an executive of the law.

Miss Woppit, though hardly reassured by the hearty protestations of Hoover and Barber Sam as to her brother's security, hoped that all would be well. With evident diffidence she bade her guests make themselves at home; there was plenty of wood in the box behind the stove and plenty of oil in the tell tale lamp; she fetched a big platter of crackers, a mammoth cut of cheese, a can of cove oysters, and a noble supply of condiments. Did the gents reckon they would be comfortable? The gents smiled and bowed obsequiously, neither, however, indulging in conversation to any marked degree, for, as was quite natural, each felt in the presence of his rival a certain embarrassment which we can fancy Miss Woppit respected if she did not enjoy it.

Finally Miss Woppit retired to her own delectable bower in the kitchen with the parting remark that she would sleep in a sense of perfect security; this declaration flattered her protectors, albeit she had no sooner closed the door than she piled the kitchen woodbox and her own small trunk against it a proceeding that touched Three fingered Hoover deeply and evoked from him a tender expression as to the natural timidity of womankind, which sentiment the crafty Barber Sam instantly indorsed in a tone loud enough for the lady to hear.

It is presumed that Miss Woppit slept that night. Following the moving of that woodbox and that small trunk there was no sound of betrayal if Miss Woppit did not sleep. Once the men in the front room were startled by the woman's voice crying out, "Jim oh, Jim!" in tones of such terror as to leave no doubt that Miss Woppit slept and dreamed frightful dreams.

The men themselves were wakeful enough; they were there to protect a lady, and they were in no particular derelict to that trust. Sometimes they talked together in the hushed voices that beseem a sick chamber; anon they took up their music apparata and thrummed and sawed therefrom such harmonies as would seem likely to lull to sweeter repose the object of their affection in the adjoining chamber beyond the woodbox and the small trunk; the circumstance of the robbery they discussed in discreet tones, both agreeing that the highwaymen were as good as dead by this time. We can fancy that the twain were distinctly annoyed upon discovering in one corner of the room, during their vigils, a number of Leadville and Denver newspapers containing sonnets, poems, odes, triolets, and such like, conspicuously marked with blue or red pencil tracings and all aimed, in a poetic sense, at Miss Woppit's virgin heart. This was the subtle work of the gifted Jake Dodsley! This was his ingenious way of storming the citadel of the coy maiden's affections.

The discovery led Barber Sam to ventilate his opinion of the crafty Dodsley, an opinion designedly pitched in a high and stentorian key and expressive of everything but compliment. On the contrary, Three fingered Hoover a guileless man, if ever there was one stood bravely up for Jake, imputing this artifice of his to a passion which knows no ethics so far as competition is concerned. It was true, as Hoover admitted, that poets seldom make good husbands, but, being an exceptionally good poet,

Jake might prove also an exception in matrimony, providing he found a wife at his time of life. But as to the genius of the man there could be no question; not even the poet Pabor had in all his glory done a poem so fine as that favorite poem of Hoover's, which, direct from the burning types of the "Leadville Herald," Hoover had committed to the tablets of his memory and was wont to repeat or sing on all occasions to the aggrandizement of Jake Dodsley's fame. Gradually the trend of the discussion led to the suggestion that Hoover sing this favorite poem, and this he did in a soothing, soulful voice. Barber Sam accompanying him upon that wondrous guitar. What a picture that must have been! Even upon the mountain sides of that far off West human hearts respond tenderly to the touch of love.

Wot though time flies?
Turrue love never dies!

That honest voice oh, could I hear it now! That honest face oh, could I see it again! And, oh, that once more I could feel the clasp of that brave hand and the cordial grace of that dear, noble presence!

It was in the fall of the year; the nights were long, yet this night sped quickly. Long before daybreak significant sounds in the back room betokened that Miss Woppit was up and moving around. Through the closed door and from behind the improvised rampart of wood box and small trunk the young lady informed her chivalric protectors that they might go home, prefacing this permission, however, with a solicitous inquiry as to whether anything had been heard from Brother Jim and his posse.

Jim Woppit and his men must have had a hard ride of it. They did not show up in camp until eleven o'clock that day, and a tougher looking outfit you never saw. They had scoured the surrounding country with the utmost diligence, yet no trace whatever had they discovered of the outlaws; the wretches had disappeared so quickly, so mysteriously, that it seemed hard to believe that they had indeed existed. The crime, so boldly and so successfully done, was of course the one theme of talk, of theory, and of speculation in all that region for the conventional period of nine days. And then it appeared to be forgotten, or, at least, men seldom spoke of it, and presently it came to be accepted as the popular belief that the robbery had been committed by a gang of desperate tramps, this theory being confirmed by a certain exploit subsequently in the San Juan country, an exploit wherein three desperate tramps assaulted the triweekly road hack, and, making off with their booty, were ultimately taken and strung up to a convenient tree.

Still, the reward of one thousand dollars offered by the city government of Red Hoss Mountain for information leading to the arrest of the glen robbers was not withdrawn, and there were those in the camp who quietly persevered in the belief that the outrage had been done by parties as yet undiscovered, if not unsuspected. Mr. Mills, the superintendent of the Royal Victoria, had many a secret conference with Jim Woppit, and it finally leaked out that the cold, discriminating, and vigilant eye of eternal justice was riveted upon Steve Barclay, the stage driver. Few of us suspected Steve; he was a good natured, inoffensive fellow; it seemed the idlest folly to surmise that he could have been in collusion with the highwaymen. But Mr. Mills had his own ideas on the subject; he was a man of positive convictions, and, having pretty nearly always demonstrated that he was in the right, it boded ill for Steve Barclay when Mr. Mills made up his mind that Steve must have been concerned in one way or another in that Magpie Glen crime.

The wooing of Miss Woppit pursued the even tenor of its curious triple way. Wars and rumors of wars served merely to imbue it with certain heroic fervor. Jake Dodsley's contributions to the "Leadville Herald" and to Henry Feldwisch's Denver "Inter Ocean," though still aimed at the virgin mistress of The Bower, were pitched in a more exalted key and breathed a spirit that defied all human dangers. What though death confronted the poet and the brutal malice of nocturnal marauders threatened the object of his adoration, what, short of superhuman intervention, should prevent the poet from baffling all hostile environments and placing the queen of his heart securely upon his throne beside him, etc., etc.? We all know how the poets go it when they once get started. The Magpie Glen affair gave Jake Dodsley a new impulse, and marked copies of his wonderful effusions found their way to the Woppit cabin in amazing plenty and with exceeding frequency. In a moment of vindictive bitterness was Barber Sam heard to intimate that the robbery was particularly to be regretted for having served to open the sluices of Jake Dodsley's poetic soul.

'T was the purest comedy, this wooing was; through it all the finger of fate traced a deep line of pathos. The poetic Dodsley, with his inexhaustible fund of rhyme, of optimism and of subtlety; Barber Sam, with his envy, his jealousy, and his garrulity; Three fingered Hoover with his manly yearning, timorousness, tenderness, and awkwardness these three in a seemingly vain quest of love reciprocated; the girl, fair, lonely, dutiful filled with devotion to her brother and striving, amid it all, to preserve a proper womanly neutrality toward these other men; there was in this little comedy among those distant hills so much of real pathos.

As for Jim Woppit, he showed not the slightest partiality toward any one of the three suitors; with all he was upon terms of equal friendship. It seemed as if Jim had made up his mind in the beginning to let the best one win; it was a free, fair, square race, so far as Jim was concerned, and that was why Jim always had stanch backers in Jake Dodsley, Barber Sam, and Three fingered Hoover.

My sympathies were all with Hoover; he and I were pardners. He loved the girl in his own beautiful, awkward way. He seldom spoke of her to me, for he was not the man to unfold what his heart treasured. He was not an envious man, yet sometimes he would tell how he regretted that early education had not fallen to his lot, for in that case he, too, might have been a poet. Mother the old red fiddle was his solace. Coming home to our cabin late of nights I'd hear him within scraping away at that tune De Blanc had written for him, and he believed what Mother sung to him in her squeaky voice of the deathlessness of true love. And many a time I can tell it now many a time in the dead of night I have known him to steal out of the cabin with Mother and go up the main road to the gateway of The Bower, where, in moonlight or in darkness (it mattered not to him), he would repeat over and over again that melancholy tune, hoping thereby to touch the sensibilities of the lady of his heart.

In the early part of February there was a second robbery. This time the stage was overhauled at Lone Pine, a ranch five miles beyond the camp. The details of this affair were similar to those of the previous business in the glen. A masked man sprang from the roadside, presented two revolvers at Steve Barclay's head, and called upon all within the stage to come out, holding up their hands. The outrage was successfully carried out, but the booty was inconsiderable, somewhat less than eight hundred dollars falling into the highwayman's hands. The robber and his pals fled as before; the time that elapsed before word could be got to camp facilitated the escape of the outlaws.

A two days' scouring of the surrounding country revealed absolutely no sign or trace of the fugitives. But it was pretty evident now that the two crimes had been committed by a gang intimately acquainted with, if not actually living in, the locality. Confirmation of this was had when five weeks later the stage was again stopped and robbed at Lone Pine under conditions exactly corresponding with the second robbery. The mystery baffled the wits of all. Intense excitement prevailed; a reward of five thousand dollars was advertised for the apprehension of the outlaws; the camp fairly seethed with rage, and the mining country for miles around was stirred by a determination to hunt out and kill the miscreants. Detectives came from Denver and snooped around. Everybody bought extra guns and laid in a further supply of ammunition. Yet the stage robbers bless you! nobody could find hide or hair of 'em.

Miss Woppit stood her share of the excitement and alarm as long as she could, and then she spoke her mind to Jim. He told us about it. Miss Woppit owed a certain duty to Jim, she said; was it not enough for her to be worried almost to death with fears for his safety as marshal of the camp? Was it fair that in addition to this haunting terror she should be constantly harassed by a consciousness of her own personal danger? She was a woman and alone in a cabin some distance from any other habitation; one crime had been committed within a step of that isolated cabin; what further crime might not be attempted by the miscreants?

"The girl is skeered," said Jim Woppit, "and I don't know that I wonder at it. Women folks is nervous like, anyhow, and these doings of late hev been enough to worrit the strongest of us men."

"Why, there ain't an hour in the day," testified Casey, "that Miss Woppit don't telephone down here to ask whether everything is all right, and whether Jim is O. K."

"I know it," said Jim. "The girl is skeered, and I 'd oughter thought of it before. I must bring her down into the camp to live. Jest ez soon ez I can git the lumber I 'll put up a cabin on the Bush lot next to the bank."

Jim owned the Bush lot, as it was called. He had talked about building a store there in the spring, but we all applauded this sudden determination to put up a cabin instead, a home for his sister. That was a determination that bespoke a thoughtfulness and a tenderness that ennobled Jim Woppit in our opinions. It was the square thing.

Barber Sam, ever fertile in suggestion, allowed that it might be a pious idea for Miss Woppit to move down to the Mears House and board there until the new cabin was built. Possibly the circumstance that Barber Sam himself boarded at the Mears House did not inspire this suggestion. At any rate, the suggestion seemed a good one, but Jim duly reported that his sister thought it better to stay in the old place till the new place was ready; she had stuck it out so far, and she would try to stick it out the little while longer yet required.

This ultimatum must have interrupted the serenity of Barber Sam's temper; he broke his E string that evening, and half an hour later somebody sat down on the guitar and cracked it irremediably.

And now again it was spring. Nothing can keep away the change in the season. In the mountain country the change comes swiftly, unheralded. One day it was bleak and cheerless; the next day brought with it the grace of sunshine and warmth; as if by magic, verdure began to deck the hillsides, and we heard again the cheerful murmur of waters in the gulch. The hollyhocks about The Bower shot up once more and put forth their honest, rugged leaves. In this divine springtime, who could think evil, who do it?

Sir Charles Lackington, president of the Royal Victoria mine, was now due at the camp. He represented the English syndicate that owned the large property. Ill health compelled him to live at Colorado Springs. Once a year he visited Red Hoss Mountain, and always in May. It was announced that he would come to the camp by Tuesday's stage. That stage was robbed by that mysterious outlaw and his gang. But Sir Charles happened not to be among the passengers.

This robbery (the fourth altogether) took place at a point midway between Lone Pine and the glen. The highwayman darted upon the leading horses as they were descending the hill and so misdirected their course that the coach was overturned in the brush at the roadside. In the fall Steve Barclay's right arm was broken. With consummate coolness the highwayman (now positively described as a thick set man, with a beard) proceeded to relieve his victims of their valuables, but not until he had called, as was his wont, to his confederates in ambush to keep the passengers covered with their rifles. The outlaw inquired which of his victims was Sir Charles Lackington, and evinced rage when he learned that that gentleman was not among the passengers by coach.

It happened that Jake Dodsley was one of the victims of the highwayman's greed. He had been to Denver and was bringing home a pair of elaborate gold earrings which he intended for for Miss Woppit, of course. Poets have deeper and stronger feelings than common folk. Jake Dodsley's poetic nature rebelled when he found himself deprived of those lovely baubles intended for the idol of his heart. So, no sooner had the outlaw retreated to the brush than Jake Dodsley whipped out his gun and took to the same brush, bent upon an encounter with his despoiler. Poor Jake never came from the brush alive. The rest heard the report of a rifle shot, and when, some time later, they found Jake, he was dead, with a rifle ball in his head.

The first murder done and the fourth robbery! Yet the mystery was as insoluble as ever. Of what avail was the rage of eight hundred miners, the sagacity of the indefatigable officers of the law, and the united efforts of the vengeance breathing population throughout the country round about to hunt the murderers down? Why, it seemed as if the devil himself were holding justice up to ridicule and scorn.

We had the funeral next day. Sir Charles Lackington came by private wagon in the morning; his daughter was with him. Their escape from participation in the affair of the previous day naturally filled them with thanksgiving, yet did not abate their sympathy for the rest of us in our mourning over the dead poet. Sir Charles was the first to suggest a fund for a monument to poor Jake, and he headed the subscription list with one hundred dollars, cash down. A noble funeral it was; everybody cried; at the grave Three fingered Hoover recited the poem about true love and Jim Woppit threw in a wreath of hollyhock leaves which his sister had sent the poor thing was too sick to come herself. She must have cared more for Jake than she had ever let on, for she took to her bed when she heard that he was dead.

Amid the deepest excitement further schemes for the apprehension of the criminals who had so long baffled detection were set on foot and but this is not a story of crime; it is the story of a wooing, and I must not suffer myself to be drawn away from the narrative of that wooing. With the death of the poet Dodsley one actor fell out of the little comedy. And yet another stepped in at once. You would hardly guess who it was Mary Lackington. This seventeen year old girl favored her father in personal appearance and character; she was of the English type of blonde beauty a light hearted, good hearted, sympathetic creature who recognized it as her paramount duty to minister to her invalid father. He had been her instructor in books, he had conducted her education, he had directed her amusements, he had been her associate in short, father and daughter were companions, and from that sweet companionship both derived a solace and wisdom precious above all things else. Mary Lackington was, perhaps, in some particulars mature beyond her years; the sweetness, the simplicity, and the guilelessness of her character was the sweetness, the simplicity, and the guilelessness of childhood. Fair and innocent, this womanly maiden came into the comedy of that mountain wooing.

Three fingered Hoover had never been regarded an artful man, but now, all at once, for the first time in his life, he practised a subtlety. He became acquainted with Mary Lackington; I am not sure that he did not meet Sir Charles at the firemen's muster in Pueblo some years before. Getting acquainted with Miss Mary was no hard thing; the girl flitted whithersoever she pleased, and she enjoyed chatting with the miners, whom she found charmingly fresh, original, and manly, and as for the miners, they simply adored Miss Mary. Sir Charles owed his popularity largely to his winsome daughter.

Mary was not long in discovering that Three fingered Hoover had a little romance all of his own. Maybe some of the other boys told her about it. At any rate, Mary was charmed, and without hesitation she commanded Hoover to confess all. How the big, awkward fellow ever got through with it I for my part can't imagine, but tell her he did yes, he fairly unbosomed his secret, and Mary was still more delighted and laughed and declared that it was the loveliest love story she had ever heard. Right here was where Hoover's first and only subtlety came in.

"And now, Miss Mary," says he, "you can do me a good turn, and I hope you will do it. Get acquainted with the lady and work it up with her for me. Tell her that you know not that I told you, but that you happen to have found it out, that I like her like her better 'n anybody else; that I 'm the pure stuff; that if anybody ties to me they can find me thar every time and can bet their last case on me! Don't lay it on too thick, but sort of let on I 'm O. K. You women understand such things if you 'll help me locate this claim I 'm sure everything 'll pan out all right; will ye?"

The bare thought of promoting a love affair set Mary nearly wild with enthusiasm. She had read of experiences of this kind, but of course she had never participated in any. She accepted the commission gayly yet earnestly. She would seek Miss Woppit at once, and she would be so discreet in her tactics yes, she would be as artful as the most skilled diplomat at the court of love.

Had she met Miss Woppit? Yes, and then again no. She had been rambling in the glen yesterday and, coming down the road, had stopped near the pathway leading to The Bower to pick a wild flower of exceeding brilliancy. About to resume her course to camp she became aware that another stood near her. A woman, having passed noiselessly from the cabin, stood in the gravelly pathway looking upon the girl with an expression wholly indefinable. The woman was young, perhaps twenty; she was tall and of symmetrical form, though rather stout; her face was comely, perchance a bit masculine in its strength of features, and the eyes were shy, but of swift and certain glance, as if instantaneously they read through and through the object upon which they rested.

"You frightened me," said Mary Lackington, and she had been startled, truly; "I did not hear you coming, and so I was frightened when I saw you standing there."

To this explanation the apparition made no answer, but continued to regard Mary steadfastly with the indefinable look an expression partly of admiration, partly of distrust, partly of appeal, perhaps. Mary Lackington grew nervous; she did therefore the most sensible thing she could have done under the circumstances she proceeded on her way homeward.

This, then, was Mary's first meeting with Miss Woppit. Not particularly encouraging to a renewal of the acquaintance; yet now that Mary had so delicate and so important a mission to execute she burned to know more of the lonely creature on that hill side, and she accepted with enthusiasm, as I have said, the charge committed to her by the enamored Hoover.

Sir Charles and his daughter remained at the camp about three weeks. In that time Mary became friendly with Miss Woppit, as intimate, in fact, as it was possible for anybody to become with her. Mary found herself drawn strangely and inexplicably toward the woman. The fascination which Miss Woppit exercised over her was altogether new to Mary; here was a woman of lowly birth and in lowly circumstances, illiterate, neglected, lonely, yet possessing a charm an indefinable charm which was distinct and potent, yet not to be analyzed yes, hardly recognizable by any process of cool mental dissection, but magically persuasive in the subtlety of its presence and influence. Mary had sought to locate, to diagnose that charm; did it lie in her sympathy with the woman's lonely lot, or was it the romance of the wooing, or was it the fascination of those restless, searching eyes that Mary so often looked up to find fixed upon her with an expression she could not forget and could not define?

I incline to the belief that all these things combined to constitute the charm whereof I speak. Miss Woppit had not the beauty that would be likely to attract one other own sex; she had none of the sprightliness and wit of womankind, and she seemed to be wholly unacquainted with the little arts, accomplishments and vanities in which women invariably find amusement. She was simply a strange, lonely creature who had accepted valorously her duty to minister to the comfort of her brother; the circumstances of her wooing invested her name and her lot with a certain pleasing romance; she was a woman, she was loyal to her sense of duty, and she was, to a greater degree than most women, a martyr herein, perhaps, lay the secret to the fascination Miss Woppit had for Mary Lackington.

At any rate, Mary and Miss Woppit became, to all appearances, fast friends; the wooing of Miss Woppit progressed apace, and the mystery of those Red Hoss Mountain crimes became more and but I have already declared myself upon that point and I shall say no more thereof except so far as bears directly upon my story, which is, I repeat, of a wooing, and not of crime.

Three fingered Hoover had every confidence in the ultimate success of the scheme to which Miss Mary had become an enthusiastic party. In occasional pessimistic moods he found himself compelled to confess to himself that the reports made by Miss Mary were not altogether such as would inspire enthusiasm in the bosom of a man less optimistic than he Hoover was.

To tell the truth, Mary found the task of doing Hoover's courting for him much more difficult than she had ever fancied a task of that kind could be. In spite of her unacquaintance with the artifices of the world Miss Woppit exhibited the daintiest skill at turning the drift of the conversation whenever, by the most studied tact, Mary Lackington succeeded in bringing the conversation around to a point where the virtues of Three fingered Hoover, as a candidate for Miss Woppit's esteem, could be expatiated upon. From what Miss Woppit implied rather than said, Mary took it that Miss Woppit esteemed Mr. Hoover highly as a gentleman and as a friend that she perhaps valued his friendship more than she did that of any other man in the world, always excepting her brother Jim, of course.

Miss Mary reported all this to Hoover much more gracefully than I have put it, for, being a woman, her sympathies would naturally exhibit themselves with peculiar tenderness when conveying to a lover certain information touching his inamorata.

There were two subjects upon which Miss Woppit seemed to love to hear Mary talk. One was Mary herself and the other was Jim Woppit. Mary regarded this as being very natural. Why should n't this women in exile pine to hear of the gay, beautiful world outside her pent horizon? So Mary told her all about the sights she had seen, the places she had been to, the people she had met, the books she had read, the dresses she but, no, Miss Woppit cared nothing for that kind of gossip now you 'll agree that she was a remarkable woman, not to want to hear all about the lovely dresses Mary had seen and could describe so eloquently.

Then again, as to Jim, was n't it natural that Miss Woppit, fairly wrapped up in that brother, should be anxious to hear the good opinion that other folk had of him? Did the miners like Jim, she asked what did they say, and what did Sir Charles say? Miss Woppit was fertile in questionings of this kind, and Mary made satisfactory answers, for she was sure that everybody liked Jim, and as for her father, why, he had taken Jim right into his confidence the day he came to the camp.

Sir Charles had indeed made a confidant of Jim. One day he called him into his room at the Mears House. "Mr. City Marshal," said Sir Charles, in atone that implied secrecy, "I have given it out that I shall leave the camp for home day after to morrow."

"Yes, I had heerd talk," answered Jim Woppit. "You are going by the stage."

"Certainly, by the stage," said Sir Charles, "but not day after to morrow; I go to morrow."

"To morrow, sir?"

"To morrow," repeated Sir Charles. "The coach leaves here, as I am told, at eleven o' clock. At four we shall arrive at Wolcott Siding, there to catch the down express, barring delay. I say 'barring delay,' and it is with a view to evading the probability of delay that I have given out that I am to leave on a certain day, whereas, in fact, I shall leave a day earlier. You understand?"

"You bet I do," said Jim. "You are afraid of of the robbers?"

"I shall have some money with me," answered Sir Charles, "but that alone does not make me desirous of eluding the highwaymen. My daughter a fright of that kind might lead to the most disastrous results."

"Correct," said Jim.

"So I have planned this secret departure," continued Sir Charles. "No one in the camp now knows of it but you and me, and I have a favor a distinct favor to ask of you in pursuance of this plan. It is that you and a posse of the bravest men you can pick shall accompany the coach, or, what is perhaps better, precede the coach by a few minutes, so as to frighten away the outlaws in case they may happen to be lurking in ambush."

Jim signified his hearty approval of the proposition. He even expressed a fervent hope that a rencontre with the outlaws might transpire, and then he muttered a cordial "d 'em!"

"In order, however," suggested Sir Charles, "to avert suspicion here in camp it would be wise for your men to meet quietly at some obscure point and ride together, not along the main road, but around the mountain by the Tin Cup path, coming in on the main road this side of Lone Pine ranch. You should await our arrival, and then, everything being tranquil, your posse can precede us as an advance guard in accordance with my previous suggestion."

"It might be a pious idea," said Jim, "for me to give the boys a pointer. They 'll be on to it, anyhow, and I know 'em well enough to trust 'em."

"You know your men; do as you please about apprising them of their errand," said Sir Charles. "I have only to request that you assure each that he will be well rewarded for his services."

This makes a rude break in our wooing; but I am narrating actual happenings. Poor old Hoover's subtlety all for naught, Mary's friendly offices incompleted, the pleasant visits to the cabin among the hollyhocks suspended perhaps forever, Miss Woppit's lonely lot rendered still more lonely by the departure of her sweet girl friend all this was threatened by the proposed flight for flight it was of Sir Charles and Mary Lackington.

That May morning was a glorious one. Summer seemed to have burst upon the camp and the noble mountain sentinels about it.

"We are going to day," said Sir Charles to his daughter. "Hush! not a word about it to anybody. I have reasons for wishing our departure to be secret."

"You have heard bad news?" asked Mary, quickly.

"Not at all," answered Sir Charles, smilingly. "There is absolutely no cause for alarm. We must go quietly; when we reach home I will tell you my reasons and then we will have a hearty laugh together."

Mary Lackington set about packing her effects, and all the time her thoughts were of her lonely friend in the hill side cabin. In this hour of her departure she felt herself drawn even more strangely and tenderly toward that weird, incomprehensible creature; such a tugging at her heart the girl had never experienced till now. What would Miss Woppit say what would she think? The thought of going away with never so much as a good by struck Mary Lackington as being a wanton piece of heartlessness. But she would write to Miss Woppit as soon as ever she reached home she would write a letter that would banish every suspicion of unfeelingness.

Then, too, Mary thought of Hoover; what would the big, honest fellow think, to find himself deserted in this emergency without a word of warning? Altogether it was very dreadful. But Mary Lackington was a daughter who did her father's bidding trustingly.

Three fingered Hoover went with Jim Woppit that day. There were thirteen in the posse fatal number mounted on sturdy bronchos and armed to the teeth. They knew their business and they went gayly on their way. Around the mountain and over the Tin Cup path they galloped, a good seven miles, I 'll dare swear; and now at last they met up with the main road, and at Jim Woppit's command they drew in under the trees to await the approach of the party in the stage.

Meanwhile in camp the comedy was drawing to a close. Bill Merridew drove stage that day; he was Steve Barclay's pardner pretty near the only man in camp that stood out for Steve when he was suspicioned of being in some sort of cahoots with the robbers. Steve Barclay's arm was still useless and Bill was reckoned the next best horseman in the world.

The stage drew up in front of the Mears House. Perhaps half a dozen passengers were in waiting and the usual bevy of idlers was there to watch the departure. Great was the astonishment when Sir Charles and Mary Lackington appeared and stepped into the coach. Everybody knew Sir Charles and his daughter, and, as I have told you, it had been given out that they were not to leave the camp until the morrow. Forthwith there passed around mysterious whisperings as to the cause of Sir Charles' sudden departure.

It must have been a whim on Barber Sam's part. At any rate, he issued just then from Casey's restaurant across the way, jaunty and chipper as ever. He saw Sir Charles in the stage and Bill Merridew on the box. He gave a low, significant whistle. Then he crossed the road.

"Bill," says he, quietly, "It 's a summerish day, and not feelin' just as pert as I oughter I reckon I 'll ride a right smart piece with you for my health!"

With these words Barber Sam climbed up and sat upon the box with Bill Merridew. A moment later the stage was on its course along the main road.

"Look a' here, Bill Merridew," says Barber Sam, fiercely, "there 's a lord inside and you outside, to day a mighty suspicious coincidence! No, you need n't let on you don't tumble to my meenin'! I 've had my eye on Steve Barclay an' you, and I 'm ready for a showdown. I 'm travelin' for my health to day, and so are you, Bill Merridew! I 'm fixed from the ground up an' you know there ain't a man in the Red Hoss Mountain country that is handier with a gun than me. Now I mean bizness; if there is any onpleasantness to day and if you try to come any funny bizness, why, d—me, Bill Merridew, if I don't blow your head off!"

Pleasant words these for Bill to listen to. But Bill knew Barber Sam and he had presence of mind enough to couch his expostulatory reply in the most obsequious terms. He protested against Barber Sam's harsh imputations.

"I 've had my say," was Barber Sam's answer. "I ain't goin' to rub it in. You understand that I mean bizness this trip; so don't forget it. Now let's talk about the weather."

Mary Lackington had hoped that, as they passed The Bower, she would catch a glimpse of Miss Woppit perhaps have sufficient opportunity to call out a hasty farewell to her. But Miss Woppit was nowhere to be seen. The little door of the cabin was open, so presumably the mistress was not far away. Mary was disappointed, vexed; she threw herself back and resigned herself to indignant reflections.

The stage had proceeded perhaps four miles on its way when its progress was arrested by the sudden appearance of a man, whose habit and gestures threatened evil. This stranger was of short and chunky build and he was clad in stout, dark garments that fitted him snugly. A slouch hat was pulled down over his head and a half mask of brown muslin concealed the features of his face. He held out two murderous pistols and in a sharp voice cried "Halt!" Instantaneously Barber Sam recognized in this bold figure the mysterious outlaw who for so many months had been the terror of the district, and instinctively he reached for his pistol pocket.

"Throw up your hands!" commanded the outlaw. He had the drop on them. Recalling poor Jake Dodsley's fate Barber Sam discreetly did as he was bidden. As for Bill Merridew, he was shaking like a wine jelly. The horses had come to a stand, and the passengers in the coach were wondering why a stop had been made so soon. Wholly unaware of what had happened, Mary Lackington thrust her head from the door window of the coach and looked forward up the road, in the direction of the threatening outlaw. She comprehended the situation at once and with a scream fell back into her father's arms.

Presumably, the unexpected discovery of a woman among the number of his intended victims disconcerted the ruffian. At any rate, he stepped back a pace or two and for a moment lowered his weapons. That moment was fatal to him. Quick as lightning Barber Sam whipped out his unerring revolver and fired. The outlaw fell like a lump of dough in the road. At that instant Bill Merridew recovered his wits; gathering up the lines and laying on the whip mercilessly he urged his horses into a gallop. Over the body of the outlaw crunched the hoofs of the frightened brutes and rumbled the wheels of the heavy stage.

"We 've got him this time!" yelled Barber Sam, wildly. "Stop your horses, Bill you 're all right, Bill, and I 'm sorry I ever did you dirt stop your horses, and let 's finish the sneakin' critter!"

There was the greatest excitement. The passengers fairly fell out of the coach, and it seemed as if they had an arsenal with them. Mary Lackington was as self possessed as any of the rest.

"Are you sure he is dead?" she asked. "Don't let us go nearer till we know that he is dead; he will surely kill us!"

The gamest man in the world would n't have stood the ghost of a show in the face of those murderous weapons now brought to bear on the fallen and crushed wretch.

"If he ain't dead already he 's so near it that there ain't no fun in it," said Bill Merridew.

In spite of this assurance, however, the party advanced cautiously toward the man. Convinced finally that there was no longer cause for alarm, Barber Sam strode boldly up to the body, bent over it, tore off the hat and pulled aside the muslin half mask. One swift glance at the outlaw's face, and Barber Sam recoiled.

"Great God!" he cried, "Miss Woppit!"

It was, indeed, Miss Woppit the fair haired, shy eyed boy who for months had masqueraded in the camp as a woman. Now, that masquerade disclosed and the dreadful mystery of the past revealed, the nameless boy, fair in spite of his crimes and his hideous wounds, lay dying in the dust and gravel of the road.

Jim Woppit and his posse, a mile away, had heard the pistol shot. It seemed but a moment ere they swept down the road to the scene of the tragedy; they came with the swiftness of the wind. Jim Woppit galloped ahead, his swarthy face the picture of terror.

"Who is it who 's killed who 's hurt?" he asked.

Nobody made answer, and that meant everything to Jim. He leapt from his horse, crept to the dying boy's side and took the bruised head into his lap. The yellowish hair had fallen down about the shoulders; Jim stroked it and spoke to the white face, repeating "Willie, Willie, Willie," over and over again.

The presence and the voice of that evil brother, whom he had so bravely served, seemed to arrest the offices of Death. The boy came slowly to, opened his eyes and saw Jim Woppit there. There was pathos, not reproach, in the dying eyes.

"It 's all up, Jim," said the boy, faintly, "I did the best I could."

All that Jim Woppit could answer was "Willie, Willie, Willie," over and over again.

"This was to have been the last and we were going away to be decent folks," this was what the boy went on to say; "I wish it could have been so, for I have wanted to live ever since ever since I knew her."

Mary Lackington gave a great moan. She stood a way off, but she heard these words and they revealed much so very much to her more, perhaps, than you and I can guess.

He did not speak her name. The boy seemed not to know that she was there. He said no other word, but with Jim Woppit bending over him and wailing that piteous "Willie, Willie, Willie," over and over again, the boy closed his eyes and was dead.

Then they all looked upon Jim Woppit, but no one spoke. If words were to be said, it was Jim Woppit's place to say them, and that dreadful silence seemed to cry: "Speak out, Jim Woppit, for your last hour has come!"

Jim Woppit was no coward. He stood erect before them all and plucked from his breast the star of his office and cast away from him the weapon he had worn. He was magnificent in that last, evil hour!

"Men," said he. "I speak for him an' not for myself. Ez God is my judge, that boy wuz not to blame. I made him do it all the lyin', the robbery, the murder; he done it because I told him to, an' because havin' begun he tried to save me. Why, he wuz a kid ez innocent ez a leetle toddlin' child. He wanted to go away from here an' be different from wot he wuz, but I kep' at him an' made him do an' do agin wot has brought the end to day. Las' night he cried when I told him he must do the stage this mornin; seemed like he wuz soft on the girl yonder. It wuz to have been the las' time I promised him that, an' so an' so it is. Men, you 'll find the money an' everything else in the cabin under the floor of the cabin. Make it ez square all round ez you kin."

Then Jim Woppit backed a space away, and, before the rest could realize what he was about, he turned, darted through the narrow thicket, and hurled himself into the gulch, seven hundred feet down.

But the May sunlight was sweet and gracious, and there lay the dead boy, caressed of that charity of nature and smiling in its glory.

Bill was the first to speak Bill Merridew, I mean. He was Steve Barclay's partner and both had been wronged most grievously.

"Now throw the other one over, too," cried Bill, savagely. "Let 'em both rot in the gulch!"

But a braver, kindlier man said "No!" It was Three fingered Hoover, who came forward now and knelt beside the dead boy and held the white face between his hard, brown hands and smoothed the yellowish hair and looked with unspeakable tenderness upon the closed eyes.

"Leave her to me," said he, reverently. "It wuz ez near ez I ever come to lovin' a woman, and I reckon it's ez near ez I ever shell come. So let me do with her ez pleases me."

It was their will to let Three fingered Hoover have his way. With exceeding tenderness he bore the body back to camp and he gave it into the hands of womenfolk to prepare it for burial, that no man's touch should profane that vestige of his love. You see he chose to think of her to the last as she had seemed to him in life.

And it was another conceit of his to put over the grave, among the hollyhocks on that mountain side, a shaft of pure white marble bearing simply the words "Miss Woppit."

THE TALISMAN

There was a boy named Wilhelm who was the only son of a widow. He was so devoted and obedient that other people in the village used to be saying always: "What a good son Wilhelm is; how kind he is to his mother." So, while he was the example for all the other boys in the village, he was the pride of his mother, who told him that some day he would marry a princess for having been such a good and dutiful son.

When the time came for him to go out into the world and make his living, his mother blessed him and said, "Here, my son, is a talisman, which you are to hang about your neck and wear nearest your heart. Whenever you are in trouble, look at this talisman and it will preserve you from harm."

So, with his mother's kiss upon his lips and the talisman next his heart, Wilhelm set out to make his fortune in the world. The talisman was simply an old silver coin which had been smoothly polished upon one side and inscribed with the word "Mother;" yet Wilhelm prized it above all other earthly things first, because his mother had given it to him, and again because he believed it possessed a charm that would keep him from harm.

Wilhelm travelled many days through the forests and over the hills in search of a town where he might find employment, and the food with which his mother had provided him for the journey was nearly gone. But whenever he was inclined to sadness, he drew the talisman from his bosom and the sight of the name of mother restored his spirits.

One evening as he climbed a hill, he beheld a great city about a league distant.

"Here at last I shall find employment," thought he. But he had no sooner uttered these words than he heard something like a sigh issuing from the roadside and as he turned to discover whence it came, he saw a dark and forbidding looking old castle standing back some way from the road in a cluster of forest trees. The grounds belonging to this old castle were surrounded by a single fence, between the palings of which a white swan stretched out its neck and gave utterance to the sighs which had attracted Wilhelm's attention.

The dismal noise made by the bird and its strange actions for it fluttered its wings wildly and waved its head as if it would have Wilhelm approach excited Wilhelm's curiosity, and he drew nearer the fence and said, "Why do you act so strangely, white swan?"

But the swan made no answer except to sigh more dismally than before and flap its wings still more widely. Then Wilhelm saw that the swan, although a swan in every other particular, had the eyes of a human being. He had scarcely recovered from the astonishment occasioned by this discovery, when the first swan was joined by a full score of other white swans that came running over the green sward, sighing very dismally and many of them shedding tears from their human eyes.

It was only the approach of night that hastened Wilhelm on his journey to the city, and, as he trudged along, he could not help thinking of the singular adventure with the swans. Presently he came upon a countryman sitting by the roadside, and to him he told the story of the castle and the swans.

"Ah," said the countryman, "you are an innocent lad to be sure! That was the castle of the old witch, and the swans you saw are unfortunate princes whom she has enchanted."

Then Wilhelm begged him to tell him about the old witch and the poor princes, and the countryman told him all from first to last, only I will have to make it much shorter, as it was a long tale.

It seems that the old witch was once a princess who was famed for her beauty and wit. She had a younger sister who was quite as beautiful, but much more amiable and much less ambitious. These sister princesses lived in the castle together, and the elder, whose name was Mirza, guarded the younger very jealously lest the younger should be first married. One time the Prince Joseph determined he would wed. He was the handsomest and bravest prince in the land and all the princesses set their caps for him, Mirza among the others. But it came to the prince's ears that Mirza was learned in and practised witchcraft, so, despite her beauty and her grace, he would have no thought of Mirza, but chose her younger sister to wife.

When the prince wedded the younger princess, Mirza was enraged beyond all saying, and forthwith she dismissed her court and gave up her life to the singing of incantations and the dreadful practices of a witch; and so constant was she in the practice of those black arts that her back became bent, her hair white, and her face wrinkled, and she grew to be the most hideous hag in the whole kingdom. Meanwhile, the prince had become king; and his wife, the queen, had presented him with a daughter, so beautiful that her like had never been seen on earth. This little princess was named Mary, a name esteemed then, as now, as the most beautiful of all names. Mary increased in loveliness each day and when she was fifteen the fame of her beauty and amiability was worldwide.

But one day, as the princess sat counting her pearls in her chamber, the old witch Mirza flew in through the window on a broomstick and carried the princess Mary off to her forlorn old castle, a league beyond the city. The queen mother, who had witnessed this violence, fell into a swoon from which she never recovered, and the whole court was thrown into a vast commotion.

Having buried his fair queen, the bereaved king set about to recover his daughter, the princess Mary, but this was found to be impossible, since the witch had locked the girl in an upper chamber of the castle and had set a catamaran and a boogaboo to guard the place. So, whenever the king's soldiers attempted to rescue the princess, the catamaran breathed fire from his nostrils upon them while the boogaboo tore out their hearts with his fierce claws.

Finally the king sent word to the witch that he would bestow upon her all the riches of his kingdom if she would restore his daughter, but she replied that there was only one condition upon which she would give up the princess and that was that some young man of the kingdom should rightly answer three questions she would propound. At once the bravest and handsomest knights in the kingdom volunteered to rescue the princess, but having failed to answer the questions of the old witch, they were transformed into swans and were condemned to eke out miserable existences in the dreary park around the old witch's castle.

"This," said the countryman, "is the story of the princess, the witch and the swans. Every once in a while, an adventuresome youth seeks to restore the princess to her father, and he is as surely transformed into a swan. So, while the court is in mourning, the princess pines in the witch's castle and the swans wander about the castle yard."

This piteous tale awakened Wilhelm's sympathy, and although it was now quite dark, he determined to go back to the witch's castle and catch a glimpse of the beautiful princess.

"May luck attend thee," said the countryman, "but beware of the catamaran and the boogaboo."

As he was plodding back to the witch's castle, Wilhelm drew his talisman from his bosom and gazed tenderly upon it. It had never looked so bright and shining. The moon beams danced upon its smooth face and kissed it. Wilhelm was confident that this was an omen that his dear mother approved the errand he was on. Then he knelt down by the roadside and said a little prayer, and when he had finished, the night zephyrs breathed their sweetest music in his ears, and Wilhelm thought it was the heavenly Father whispering words of encouragement to him. So Wilhelm went boldly toward the witch's castle.

As he drew nigh to the castle, he saw the old witch fly away on her broomstick, accompanied by a bevy of snarling hobgoblins that were also on broomsticks and looked very hideous. Then Wilhelm knew the witch and her escort were off for the forest and would not return till midnight.

The princess Mary was standing at the barred window of her chamber and was weeping. As Wilhelm approached the castle, the swans rushed to meet him, and the flapping of their wings and their piteous cries attracted the attention of the princess, and she saw Wilhelm.

"Oh, fly from here, sweet prince," cried the princess; "for if the witch were to return, she would kill you and boil your heart in her cauldron!"

"I am no prince," replied Wilhelm, "and I do not fear the ugly old witch."

Then Wilhelm told the princess who he was and how he was ready to serve her, for, having perceived her rare beauty and amiability, he was madly in love with her and was ready to die for her sake. But the princess, who was most agreeably impressed by his manly figure, handsome face, and honest valor, begged him not to risk his life for her.

"It is better that I should pass my existence here in prison," said she, "than that you should be transformed as these other wretched princes have been."

And when they heard these words, the swans craned their necks and gave utterance to such heartrending sighs that the princess sobbed with renewed vigor and even Wilhelm fell to weeping.

At this moment, hearing the commotion in the yard, the hideous catamaran and the ugly boogaboo came out of the castle and regarded Wilhelm with ferocious countenances. Never before had Wilhelm seen such revolting monsters!

The catamaran had a body and tail like an alligator, a head like a hippopotamus, and four legs like the legs of an ostrich. The body was covered with greenish scales, its eyes were living fire, and scorching flames issued from its mouth and ears. The boogaboo was none the less frightful in its appearance. It resembled a monster ape, except that instead of a hairy hide it had a scabby skin as red as a salamander's. Its arms were long and muscular, and its bony hands were armed with eleven fingers each, upon which were nails or claws shaped like fish hooks and keen as razors. This boogaboo had skinny wings like a huge bat, and at the end of its rat like tail was a sting more deadly than the poison of a snake.

These hideous reptiles the catamaran and the boogaboo stood glaring at Wilhelm.

"Ow wow wow wow!" roared the catamaran; "I will scorch you to a cinder."

"Ow wow wow wow!" bellowed the boogaboo, "I will tear your heart from your bosom."

So, in the wise determination not to die until he had made a brave and discreet struggle for the princess, Wilhelm left the castle and stole down the highway towards the city.

That night he slept in a meadow, and the stars watched over him and the daisies and buttercups bent their heads lovingly above him and sang lullabies, while he dreamed of his mother and the princess, who seemed to smile upon him all that night.

In the morning, Wilhelm pushed on to the city, and he went straight to the palace gate and demanded to see the king. This was no easy matter, but finally he was admitted and the king asked him what he wanted. When the king heard that Wilhelm was determined to make an attempt to rescue the princess, he burst out crying and embracing the youth, assured him that it was folly for him a simple country boy to undertake to accomplish what so many accomplished and skilled princes had essayed in vain.

But Wilhelm insisted, until at last the king called his court together and announced that the simple country lad had resolved to guess the riddles of the old witch. The courtiers straightway fell to laughing at the presumption of the rural wight, as they derisively called him, but it was much to the credit of the court ladies that they admired the youth for his comely person, ingenuous manners, and brave determination. The end of it all was that, at noon that very day, a long procession went with Wilhelm to the witch's castle, the courtiers hardly suppressing their mirth, but the ladies all in tears for fear the handsome youth would not guess the riddles and would therefore be transformed by the witch.

The old witch saw the train approaching her castle and she went out into the yard and sat on a rickety bench under a upas tree to receive the king and his court. She was attended by twelve snapdragons, a score of hobgoblins, and innumerable gnomes, elves, ghouls, and hoodoos. On her left stood the catamaran, and on her right the boogaboo, each more revoltingly hideous than ever before.

When the king and Wilhelm and the rest of the cavalcade came into the castle yard and stood before the witch, she grinned and showed her black gums and demanded to know why they had come.

"We have a youth here who would solve your three riddles," said the king.

Then the old witch laughed, "Ha, ha, ha!" and the gnomes, ghouls, and all the rest of the enchantress' followers took up the refrain and laughed till the air was very dense with sulphurous fumes.

"Well, if the youth is resolved, let him see the doom that awaits him," said the witch, and she waved her stick.

Forthwith a strange procession issued from the castle. First came two little imps, then came two black demons, and last of all the swans, two by two, mournfully flapping their wings and giving utterance to sighs and moans more dismal than any sounds ever before heard.

"You are going to have a new companion, my pretty pets," said the old witch to the swans, whereupon the swans moaned and sighed with renewed vigor.

The king and his court trembled and wept at the spectacle, for in these unhappy birds they recognized the poor princes who had fallen victims to the foul witch's arts. To add to the misery of the scene, the beautiful princess Mary appeared at the barred window of her chamber in the castle and stretched out her white arms beseechingly. But the king and his court could avail her nothing, for the hideous catamaran and the cruel boogaboo were prepared to pounce upon and destroy whosoever attempted to rescue the unhappy maiden by violence.

"Let the presumptuous youth stand before me," cried the witch. And Wilhelm strode boldly to the open spot between the witch and the kingly retinue.

"A fine, plump swan will you make," hissed the old witch. "Now can you tell me what is sweeter than the kiss of the princess' mother?"

Now the witch had supposed that Wilhelm would reply "The kiss of the princess herself," for this was the reply that all the other youths had made. But Wilhelm made no such answer. He faced the old witch boldly and replied, "The kiss of my own mother!"

And hearing this, which was the correct answer, the witch quivered with astonishment and rage, and the catamaran fell down upon the grass and vomited its flaming breath upon itself until it was utterly consumed. So that was the last of the hideous catamaran.

"Having said that, he will not think to repeat it," thought the old witch, and she propounded the second question, which was: "What always lieth next a good man's heart?"

Now for a long time Wilhelm paused in doubt, and the king and his retinue began to tremble and the poor swans dolorously flapped their wings and sighed more piteously. But the old witch chuckled and licked her warty chops and muttered, "He will have feathers all over his back presently."

And in his doubt Wilhelm remembered the words of his dear mother: "Whenever in trouble, look at the talisman and it will preserve you from harm." So Wilhelm put his hand in his bosom and drew forth the talisman, and lo! the inscription seemed to burn itself into his very soul. Gently he raised the talisman to his lips and reverently he kissed it. And then he uttered the sacred name, "Mother."

And straightway the hideous boogaboo fell down upon the grass and with its cruel talons tore out its own heart, so that the boogaboo perished miserably in the sight of all. The old witch cowered and foamed at her ugly black mouth and uttered fearful curses and imprecations.

It was never known what the third and last riddle was, for as soon as they saw her deprived of her twin guardians, the catamaran and the boogaboo, the king's swordsmen fell upon the witch and hewed off her head, and the head and body tumbled to the ground. At that very instant the earth opened and, with a sickening groan, swallowed up the dead witch and all her elves, gnomes, imps, ghouls, snapdragons, and demons. But the swans were instantaneously transformed back into human beings, for as soon as the witch died, all enchantment over them was at an end, and there was great joy.

The recovery of the beautiful princess Mary was easily accomplished now, and the next day she was wedded to Wilhelm amid great rejoicing, the rescued princes serving as the bridegroom's best men. The king had it proclaimed that Wilhelm should be his successor, and there was great rejoicing in all the kingdom.

In the midst of his prosperity, Wilhelm did not forget his dear old mother. He sent for her at once, and she lived with Wilhelm and his bride in the splendid palace, and she was always very particular to tell everybody what a good, kind, and thoughtful son Wilhelm had always been.

Dear little boys, God has put into your bosoms a talisman which will always tell you that love of mother is the sweetest and holiest of all human things. Treasure that sacred talisman, and heaven's blessings will be always with you. And then each of you shall marry a beautiful princess, or at least one who is every whit as good as a beautiful princess.

GEORGE'S BIRTHDAY

Lawrence seemed to be lost in meditation. He sat in a rude arm chair under his favorite fig tree, and his eyes were fixed intently upon the road that wound away from the manor house, through the broad gate, and across the brown sward until it lost itself in the oak forest yonder. Had it been summer the sight of Lawrence in the arm chair under the fig tree would not have been surprising, but the spectacle of Lawrence occupying that seat in mid winter, with his gaze riveted on the sear roadway, was simply preposterous, as you will all admit.

It was a February morning clear, bright, and beautiful, with a hint of summer in the warmth of its breath and the cheeriness of its smile. Pope's Creek, as it rippled along, made pleasant music, the partridges drummed in the under brush, and the redbirds whistled weirdly in the leafless chestnut grove near the swash. Now and then a Bohemian crow, moping lazily from the Maryland border, looked down at Lawrence in the old arm chair and uttered a hoarse exclamation of astonishment.

But Lawrence heard none of these things; with stony stare he continued to regard the roadway to the grove. Could it be that he was unhappy? He was the proprietor of "Wakefield," the thirteen hundred acres that stretched around him; five hundred slaves called him master; bounteous crops had filled his barns to overflowing, and, to complete what should have been the sum of human happiness, he had but two years before taken to wife the beautiful Mary, daughter of Joseph Ball, Esq., of Epping Forest, and the acknowledged belle of the Northern Neck. How, then, could Lawrence be unhappy?

The truth is, Lawrence was in a delirium of expectancy. He stood, as it were, upon the threshold of an event. The experience which threatened him was altogether a new one; he was in a condition of suspense that was simply torturesome.

This event had been anticipated for some time. By those subtile methods peculiar to her sex, Mary, the wife, had prepared herself for it, and Lawrence, too, had declared ever and anon his readiness to face the ordeal; but, now that the event was close at hand, Lawrence was weak and nervous and pale, and it was evident that Mary would have to confront the event without the hope of any practical assistance from her husband.

"It is all the fault of the moon," muttered Lawrence. "It changed last night, and if I had paid any attention to what Aunt Lizzie and Miss Bettie said I might have expected this trouble to day. A plague take the moon, I say, and all the ills it brings with its monkeyshines!"

Along the pathway across the meadow meandered three feminine figures attired in the quaint raiment of those remote Colonial times Mistress Carter, her daughter Mistress Fairfax, and another neighbor, the antique and angular Miss Dorcas Culpeper, spinster. At sight of Lawrence they groaned, and Miss Culpeper found it necessary to hold her big velvet bag before her face to conceal the blushes of indignation which she felt suffusing her venerable features when she beheld the horrid author of a kind of trouble to which, on account of her years and estate, she could never hope to contribute save as a party of the third part. And oh! how guilty Lawrence looked and how guilty he felt, too, as he sat under his fig tree just then. He dropped his face into his hands and ground his elbows into his knees and indulged in bitter thoughts against the feminine sex in general and against the moon and Miss Dorcas Culpeper, spinster, in particular.

So absorbing were these bitter reflections that, although Lawrence had posted himself under the fig tree for the sole purpose of discovering and of heralding the approach of a certain expected visitor, he was not aware of Dr. Parley's arrival until that important personage had issued from the oak grove, had traversed the brown road, and was dignifiedly stalking his flea bitten mare through the gateway. Then Lawrence looked up, gave a sickly smile, and bade the doctor an incoherent good morning. Dr. Parley was sombre and impressive. He seldom smiled. An imperturbable gravity possessed him from the prim black satin cockade on his three cornered hat to the silver buckles on his square toed shoes. In his right hand he carried a gold headed cane which he wielded as solemnly as a pontiff might wield a sceptre, and as he dismounted from his flea bitten mare and unswung his ponderous saddlebags he never once suffered the gold head of his impressive cane to lapse from its accustomed position at his nostrils.

"Go right into the house, doctor," said Lawrence, feebly, "I 'll look after the mare. You have n't come any too soon Mary 's taking on terrible."

It was mean of Dr. Parley, but at this juncture he did really smile yes, and it was a smile which combined so much malevolent pity and scorn and derision that poor Lawrence felt himself shrivelling up to the infinitesimal dimension of a pea in a bushel basket. He led the flea bitten mare to the cherry tree and tied her there. "If you bark that tree I 'll tan you alive," said Lawrence hoarsely, to the champing, frisky creature, for now he hated all animal life from Dr. Parley down, down, down even to the flea bitten mare. Then, miserable and nervous, Lawrence returned to the arm chair under the fig tree and, how wretched he was!

Pretty soon he heard a merry treble voice piping out: "Is ze gockter tum to oo house?" and Lawrence saw little Martha toddling toward him. Little Martha was Mistress Dandridge's baby girl. The Dandridges lived a short way beyond the oak grove, and little Martha loved to visit Uncle Lawrence and Aunt Mary, as she called Lawrence and his wife.

"Yes, Martha," said Lawrence, sadly, "the doctor's come."

"Ain't oo glad ze gockter's tum?" asked the child, anxiously, for she recognized the weary tone of Lawrence's voice.

"Oh, yes," he answered, quickly and with an effort at cheerfulness, "I 'm glad he 's come. Ha, ha!"

"Is oo doing to have oo toof pulled?" she inquired, artlessly.

Lawrence shook his head.

"No, little one," said he, in a melancholy voice, "I wish I was."

Then Martha wanted to know whether the doctor had brought his saddlebags, and when Lawrence answered in the affirmative a summer of sunshine seemed to come into the child's heart and burst out over her pretty face.

"Oh, I know!" she cried, as she clapped her fat little hands. "Ze gockter has bwought oo a itty baby!"

Now Martha's innocence, naïveté, and exuberance rather pleased Lawrence. In fact, Martha was the only human being in all the world who had treated Lawrence with any kind of consideration that February morning, and all at once Lawrence felt his heart warm and go out toward the prattling child.

"Come here, little Martha," said he, kindly, "and let me hold you on my knee. Who told you about the about the the baby, eh?"

"Mamma says ze gockter allers brings itty babies in his sagglebags. Do oo want a itty baby, Uncle Lawrence?"

"Yes, Martha, I do," said he, kissing her, "and I want a little girl just like you."

Now Martha had guessed at the event, and her guess was eminently correct. Lawrence had told the truth, too; it was a little girl he wanted not one that looked like Martha, perhaps one that looked like his Mary would please him most. So the two talked together, and Lawrence found himself concocting the most preposterous perjuries touching the famous saddlebags and the babies, but it seemed to delight little Martha all the more as these perjuries became more and more preposterous.

For reasons, however, which we at this subsequent period can appreciate, this confabulation could not last for aye, and when, finally, little Martha trotted back homeward Lawrence bethought himself it was high time to reconnoiter the immediate scene of action within his house. He found a group of servants huddled about the door. Chloe, Becky, Ann, Snowdrop, Pearl, Susan, Tilly all, usually cheerful and smiling, wore distressful countenances now. Nor did they speak to him as had been their wont. They seemed to be afraid of him, yet what had he done what had he ever done that these well fed, well treated slaves should shrink from him in his hour of trouble?

It was still gloomier inside the house. Aunt Lizzie and Miss Bettie, the nurses, had taken supreme charge of affairs. At this moment Aunt Lizzie, having brewed a pot of tea, was regaling Mistress Carter and Mistress Fairfax and the venerable Miss Dorcas Culpeper, spinster, with a desultory but none the less interesting narrative of her performances on countless occasions similar to the event about to take place. The appearance of Lawrence well nigh threw Miss Culpeper into hysterics, and, to escape the dismal groans, prodigious sighs, and reproachful glances of the others, Lawrence made haste to get out of the apartment. The next room was desolate enough, but it was under Mary's room and there was some comfort in knowing that. Yet the nearer Lawrence came to Mary's room the more helpless he grew. He could not explain it, but he was lamentably weak and miserable. A strange fear undid him and he fairly trembled.

"I will go up and ask if there is anything I can do," he said to himself, for he was ashamed to admit his cowardice.

But his knees failed him and he sat down on the stairs and listened and wished he had never been born.

Oh, how quiet the house was. Lawrence strained his ears to catch a sound from Mary's room. He could hear a faint echo of the four chattering women in the front chamber below, but not a sound from Mary's room. Now and then a shrill cry of a jay or the lowing of the oxen in the pasture by the creek came to him from the outside world but not a sound from Mary's room. His heart sank; he would have given the finest plantation in Westmoreland County for the echo of Mary's voice or the music of Mary's footfall now.

Presently the door of Mary's room opened. The cold, unrelenting, forbidding countenance of Miss Bettie, the nurse, confronted Lawrence's upturned, pleading face.

"Oh, it 's you, is it?" said Miss Bettie, unfeelingly, and with this cheerless remark she closed the door again, and Lawrence was more miserable than ever. He stole down stairs into a back room, escaped through a window, and slunk away toward the stables. The whole world seemed turned against him in the flower of early manhood he found himself unwillingly and undeservedly an Ishmaelite.

He rebelled against this cruel injustice.

Then he grew weak and childish again.

Anon he anathematized humanity, and then again he ruefully regretted his own existence.

In a raging fever one moment, he shivered and chattered like a sick magpie the next.

But when he thought of Mary his heart softened and sweeter emotions thrilled him. She, at least, he assured himself, would defend him from these persecutions were she aware of them. So, after roaming aimlessly between the barn and the creek, the creek and the overseer's house, the overseer's house and the swash, the swash and the grove, the grove and the servants' quarters, Lawrence made up his mind that he 'd go back to the house (like the brave man he wanted to make himself believe he was) and help Mary endure "the ordeal," as Miss Dorcas Culpeper, spinster, was pleased to term the event. But Lawrence could not bring himself to face the feminine quartet in the front chamber now that he came to think of it he recollected that he always had detested those four impertinent gossips! So he crept around to the side window, raised it softly, crawled in through, and slipped noiselessly toward the stairway.

Then all at once he heard a cry; a shrill little voice that did not linger in his ears, but went straight to his heart and kept echoing there and twining itself in and out, in and out, over and over again.

This little voice stirred Lawrence strangely; it seemed to tell him things he had never known before, to speak a wisdom he had never dreamed of, to breathe a sweeter music than he had ever heard, to inspire ambitions purer and better than any he had ever felt the voice of his firstborn you know, fathers, what that meant to Lawrence.

Well, Lawrence was brave again, but there was a lump in his throat and his eyes were misty.

"She's here at last," he murmured thankfully; "heaven be praised for that!"

Of course you understand that Lawrence had been hoping for a girl; so had his wife. They had planned to call her Mary, after her mother, the quondam belle of the Northern Neck. Grandfather Joseph Ball, late of Epping Forest, was to be her godfather, and Colonel Bradford Custis of Jamestown had promised to grace the christening with his imposing presence.

"Well, you can come in," said Miss Bettie, with much condescension, and in all humility Lawrence did go in.

Dr. Parley was quite as solemn and impressive as ever. He occupied the great chair near the chimney place, and he still held the gold head of his everlasting cane close to his nose.

"Well, Mary," said Lawrence, with an inquiring, yearning glance. Mary was very pale, but she smiled sweetly.

"Lawrence, it's a boy," said Mary.

Oh, what a grievous disappointment that was! After all the hopes, the talk, the preparations, the plans a boy! What would Grandfather Ball, late of Epping Forest, say? What would come of the grand christening that was to be graced by the imposing presence of Colonel Bradford Custis of Jamestown? How the Jeffersons and Randolphs and Masons and Pages and Slaughters and Carters and Ayletts and Henrys would gossip and chuckle, and how he Lawrence would be held up to the scorn and the derision of the facetious yeomen of Westmoreland! It was simply terrible.

And just then, too, Lawrence's vexation was increased by a gloomy report from the four worthy dames down stairs viz., Mistress Carter, Mistress Fairfax, Miss Dorcas Culpeper, spinster, and Aunt Lizzie, the nurse. These inquiring creatures had been casting the new born babe's horoscope through the medium of tea grounds in their blue china cups, and each agreed that the child's future was full of shame, crime, disgrace, and other equally unpleasant features.

"Now that it's a boy," said Lawrence, ruefully, "I 'm willing to believe almost anything. It would n't surprise me at all if he wound up on the gallows!"

But Mary, cherishing the puffy, fuzzy, red faced little waif in her bosom, said to him, softly: "No matter what the others say, my darling; I bid you welcome, and, by God's grace, my love and prayers shall make you good and great."

And it was even so. Mary's love and prayers did make a good and great man of that unwelcome child, as we who celebrate his birthday in these later years believe. They had a grand christening, too; Grandfather Ball was there, and Colonel Bradford Custis, and the Lees, the Jeffersons, the Randolphs, the Slaughters yes, all the old families of Virginia were represented, and there was feasting and merry making for three days! Such cheer prevailed, in fact, that even Miss Dorcas Culpeper, spinster, and Lawrence, the happy father, became completely reconciled. Soothed by the grateful influences of barbecued meats and draughts of rum and sugar, Lawrence led Miss Culpeper through the minuet.

"A very proper name for the babe?" suggested Miss Culpeper.

"Yes, we will call him George, in honor of his majesty our king," said Lawrence Washington, with the pride that comes of loyalty and patriotism.

SWEET ONE DARLING AND THE DREAM FAIRIES

A wonderful thing happened one night; those who never heard of it before will hardly believe it. Sweet One Darling was lying in her little cradle with her eyes wide open, and she was trying to make up her mind whether she should go to sleep or keep awake. This is often a hard matter for little people to determine. Sweet One Darling was ready for sleep and dreams; she had on her nightgown and her nightcap, and her mother had kissed her good night. But the day had been so very pleasant, with its sunshine and its play and its many other diversions, that Sweet One Darling was quite unwilling to give it up. It was high time for the little girl to be asleep; the robins had ceased their evening song in the maple; a tree toad croaked monotonously outside, and a cricket was chirping certain confidences to the strange shadows that crept furtively everywhere in the yard and garden. Some folk believe that the cricket is in league with the Dream Fairies; they say that what sounds to us like a faint chirping merely is actually the call of the cricket to the Dream Fairies to let those pretty little creatures know that it is time for them to come with their dreams. I more than half believe this myself, for I have noticed that it is while the cricket is chirping that the Dream Fairies come with their wonderful sights that seem oftentimes very real.

Sweet One Darling heard the voice of the cricket, and may be she knew what it meant. There are a great many things which Sweet One Darling knows all about but of which she says nothing to other people; although she is only a year old, she is undoubtedly the most knowing little person in all the world, and the fact that she is the most beautiful and the most amiable of human beings is the reason why she is called by that name of Sweet One Darling. May be and it is quite likely that with all the other wonderful things she knew, Sweet One Darling understood about the arrangement that existed between the cricket and the Dream Fairies. At any rate, just as soon as she heard that cricket give its signal note she smiled a smile of gratification and looked very wise, indeed as much as to say: "The cricket and I know a thing worth knowing."

Then, all of a sudden, there was a faint sound as of the rustle of gossamer, silken wings, and the very next moment two of the cunningest fairies you ever saw were standing upon the window sill, just over the honeysuckle. They had come from Somewhere, and it was evident that they were searching for somebody, for they peered cautiously and eagerly into the room. One was dressed in a bright yellow suit of butterfly silk and the other wore a suit of dark gray mothzine, which (as perhaps you know) is a dainty fabric made of the fine strands which gray moths spin. Each of these fairies was of the height of a small cambric needle and both together would not have weighed much more than the one sixteenth part of four dewdrops. You will understand from this that these fairies were as tiny creatures as could well be imagined.

"Sweet One Darling! oh, Sweet One Darling!" they cried softly. "Where are you?"

Sweet One Darling pretended that she did not hear, and she cuddled down close in her cradle and laughed heartily, all to herself. The mischievous little thing knew well enough whom they were calling, and I am sure she knew what they wanted. But she meant to fool them and hide from them awhile that is why she did not answer. But nobody can hide from the Dream Fairies, and least of all could Sweet One Darling hide from them, for presently her laughter betrayed her and the two Dream Fairies perched on her cradle one at each side and looked smilingly down upon her.

"Hullo!" said Sweet One Darling, for she saw that her hiding place was discovered. This was the first time I had ever heard her speak, and I did not know till then that even wee little babies talk with fairies, particularly Dream Fairies.

"Hullo, Sweet One Darling!" said Gleam o' the Murk, for that was the name of the Dream Fairy in the dark gray mothzine.

"And hullo from me, too!" cried Frisk and Glitter, the other visitor the one in the butterfly silk suit.

"You have come earlier than usual," suggested Sweet One Darling.

"No, indeed," answered Frisk and Glitter; "this is the accustomed hour, but the day has been so happy that it has passed quickly. For that reason you should be glad to see me, for I bring dreams of the day the beautiful golden day, with its benediction of sunlight, its grace of warmth, and its wealth of mirth and play."

"And I," said Gleam o' the Murk, "I bring dreams, too. But my dreams are of the night, and they are full of the gentle, soothing music of the winds, of the pines, and of the crickets! and they are full of fair visions in which you shall see the things of Fairyland and of Dreamland and of all the mysterious countries that compose the vast world of Somewhere away out beyond the silvery mist of Night."

"Dear me!" cried Sweet One Darling. "I should never be able to make a choice between you two, for both of you are equally acceptable. I am sure I should love to have the pleasant play of the daytime brought back to me, and I am quite as sure that I want to see all the pretty sights that are unfolded by the dreams which Gleam o' the Murk brings."

Sweet One Darling was so distressed that her cunning little underlip drooped and quivered perceptibly. She feared that her indecision would forfeit her the friendship of both the Dream Fairies.

"You have no need to feel troubled," said Frisk and Glitter, "for you are not expected to make any choice between us. We have our own way of determining the question, as you shall presently understand."

Then the Dream Fairies explained that whenever they came of an evening to bring their dreams to a little child they seated themselves on the child's eyelids and tried to rock them down. Gleam o' the Murk would sit and rock upon one eyelid and Frisk and Glitter would sit and rock on the other. If Gleam o' the Murk's eyelid closed first the child would dream the dreams Gleam o' the Murk brought it; if Frisk and Glitter's eyelid closed first, why, then, of course, the child dreamt the dreams Frisk and Glitter brought. It would be hard to conceive of an arrangement more amicable.

"But suppose," suggested Sweet One Darling, "suppose both eyelids close at the same instant? Which one of you fairies has his own way, then?"

"Ah, in that event," said they, "neither of us wins, and, since neither wins, the sleeper does not dream at all, but awakes next morning from a sound, dreamless, refreshing sleep."

Sweet One Darling was not sure that she fancied this alternative, but of course she could not help herself. So she let the two little Dream Fairies flutter across her shoulders and clamber up her cheeks to their proper places upon her eyelids. Gracious! but how heavy they seemed when they once stood on her eyelids! As I told you before their actual combined weight hardly exceeded the sixteenth part of four dewdrops, yet when they are perched on a little child's eyelids (tired eyelids at that) it really seems sometimes as if they weighed a ton! It was just all she could do to keep her eyelids open, yet Sweet One Darling was determined to be strictly neutral. She loved both the Dream Fairies equally well, and she would not for all the world have shown either one any partiality.

Well, there the two Dream Fairies sat on Sweet One Darling's eyelids, each one trying to rock his particular eyelid down; and each one sung his little lullaby in the pipingest voice imaginable. I am not positive, but as nearly as I can remember Frisk and Glitter's song ran in this wise:

Dream, dream, dream
Of meadow, wood, and stream;
Of bird and bee,
Of flower and tree,
All under the noonday gleam;
Of the song and play

Of mirthful day
Dream, dream, dream!

This was very soothing, as you would suppose. While Frisk and Glitter sung it Sweet One Darling's eyelid drooped and drooped and drooped until, goodness me! it seemed actually closed. But at the critical moment, the other Dream Fairy, Gleam o' the Murk, would pipe up his song somewhat in this fashion:

Dream, dream, dream
Of glamour, glint, and gleam;
Of the hushaby things
The night wind sings
To the moon and the stars abeam;
Of whimsical sights
In the land o' sprites
Dream, dream, dream!

Under the spell of this pretty lullaby, the other eyelid would speedily overtake the first and so for a goodly time there was actually no such thing even as guessing which of those two eyelids would close sooner than the other. It was the most exciting contest (for an amicable one) I ever saw. As for Sweet One Darling, she seemed to be lost presently in the magic of the Dream Fairies, and although she has never said a word about it to me I am quite sure that, while her dear eyelids drooped and drooped and drooped to the rocking and the singing of the Dream Fairies, it was her lot to enjoy a confusion of all those precious things promised by her two fairy visitors. Yes, I am sure that from under her drooping eyelids she beheld the scenes of the mirthful day intermingled with peeps of fairyland, and that she heard (or seemed to hear) the music of dreamland harmonizing with the more familiar sounds of this world of ours. And when at last she was fast asleep I could not say for certain which of her eyelids had closed first, so simultaneous was the downfall of her long dark lashes upon her flushed cheeks. I meant to have asked the Dream Fairies about it, but before I could do so they whisked out of the window and away with their dreams to a very sleepy little boy who was waiting for them somewhere in the neighborhood. So you see I am unable to tell you which of the Dream Fairies won; maybe neither did; may be Sweet One Darling's sleep that night was dreamless. I have questioned her about it and she will not answer me.

This is all of the wonderful tale I had to tell. May be it will not seem so wonderful to you, for perhaps you, too, have felt the Dream Fairies rocking your eyelids down with gentle lullaby music; perhaps you, too, know all the precious dreams they bring. In that case you will bear witness that my tale, even though it be not wonderful, is strictly true.

SWEET ONE DARLING AND THE MOON GARDEN

One time Sweet One Darling heard her brother, little Our Golden Son, talking with the nurse. The nurse was a very wise woman and they called her Good Old Soul, because she was so kind to children. Little Our Golden Son was very knowing for a little boy only two years old, but there were several things he did not know about and one of these things troubled him a good deal and he went to the wise nurse to find out all about it.

"Tell me, Good Old Soul," said he, "where did I come from?"

Good Old Soul thought this a very natural question for little Our Golden Son to ask, for he was a precocious boy and was going to be a great man some time.

"I asked your mother that very question the other day," said Good Old Soul, "and what do you think she told me? She told me that the Doctor Man brought you! She told me that one night she was wishing all to herself that she had a little boy with light golden hair and dark golden eyes. 'If I had such a little boy,' said she, 'I should call him Our Golden Son.' While she was talking this way to herself, rap tap rap came a knock at the door. 'Who is there?' asked your mother. 'I am the Doctor Man,' said the person outside, 'and I have brought something for you.' Then the Doctor Man came in and he carried a box in one hand. 'I wonder what can be in the box!' thought your mother. Now what do you suppose it was?"

"Bananas?" said little Our Golden Son.

"No, no," answered Good Old Soul, "it was nothing to eat; it was the cutest, prettiest little baby boy you ever saw! Oh, how glad your mother was, and what made her particularly happy was this: The little baby boy had light golden hair and dark golden eyes! 'Did you really bring this precious little boy for me?' asked your mother. 'Indeed I did,' said the Doctor Man, and he lifted the little creature out of the box and laid him very tenderly in your mother's arms. That 's how you came, little Our Golden Son, and it was very good of the Doctor Man to bring you, was n't it?"

Little Our Golden Son was much pleased with this explanation. As for Sweet One Darling, she was hardly satisfied with what the nurse had told. So that night when the fairies the Dream Fairies came, she repeated the nurse's words to them.

"What I want to know," said Sweet One Darling, "is this: Where did the Doctor Man get little Our Golden Son? I don't doubt the truth of what Good Old Soul says, but Good Old Soul does n't tell how the Doctor Man came to have little Our Golden Son in the box. How did little Our Golden Son happen to be in the box? Where did he come from before he got into the box?"

"That is easy enough to answer," said Gleam o' the Murk. "We Dream Fairies know all about it. Before he got into the Doctor Man's box little Our Golden Son lived in the Moon. That's where all little babies live before the Doctor Man brings them."

"Did I live there before the Doctor Man brought me?" asked Sweet One Darling.

"Of course you did," said Gleam o' the Murk. "I saw you there a long, long time before the Doctor Man brought you."

"But I thought that the Moon was a big, round soda cracker," said Sweet One Darling.

That made the Dream Fairies laugh. They assured Sweet One Darling that the Moon was not a soda cracker, but a beautiful round piece of silver way, way up in the sky, and that the stars were little Moons, bearing the same relationship (in point of size) to the old mother Moon that a dime does to a big silver dollar.

"And how big is the Moon?" asked Sweet One Darling. "Is it as big as this room?"

"Oh, very, very much bigger," said the Dream Fairies.

"I guess it must be as big as a house," suggested Sweet One Darling.

"Bigger than a house," answered Gleam o' the Murk.

"Oh, my!" exclaimed Sweet One Darling, and she began to suspect that the Dream Fairies were fooling her.

But that night the Dream Fairies took Sweet One Darling with them to the Moon! You don't believe it, eh? Well, you wait until you 've heard all about it, and then, may be, you not only will believe it, but will want to go there, too.

The Dream Fairies lifted Sweet One Darling carefully out of her cradle; then their wings went "whir r r, whir r r" you 've heard a green fly buzzing against a window pane, have n't you? That was the kind of whirring noise the Dream Fairies' wings made, with the pleasing difference that the Dream Fairies' wings produced a soft, soothing music. The cricket under the honeysuckle by the window heard this music and saw the Dream Fairies carrying Sweet One Darling away. "Be sure to bring her back again," said the cricket, for he was a sociable little fellow and was very fond of little children.

You can depend upon it that Sweet One Darling had a delightful time riding through the cool night air in the arms of those Dream Fairies; it was a good deal like being a bird, only the Dream Fairies flew very much faster than any bird can fly. As they sped along they told Sweet One Darling all about the wonderful things they saw and everything was new to Sweet One Darling, for she had never made any journeys before except in the little basket carriage which Good Old Soul, her nurse, propelled every sunny morning up and down the street. Pretty soon they came to a beautiful river, which looked as if it were molten silver; but it was n't molten silver; it was a river of moonbeams.

"We will take a sail now," said Gleam o' the Murk. "This river leads straight to the Moon, and it is well worth navigating."

So they all got into a boat that had a sail made out of ten thousand and ten baby spiders' webs, and away they sailed as merrily as you please. Sweet One Darling put her feet over the side of the boat and tried to trail them in the river, but the moonbeams tickled her so that she could n't stand it very long. And what do you think? When she pulled her feet back into the boat she found them covered with dimples. She did n't know what to make of these phenomena until the Dream Fairies explained to her that a dimple always remains where a moonbeam tickles a little child. A dimple on the foot is a sure sign that one has been trailing in that beautiful silver river that leads to the Moon.

By and by they got to the Moon. I can't begin to tell you how large it was; you 'd not believe me if I did.

"This is very lovely," said Sweet One Darling, "but where are the little babies?"

"Surely you did n't suppose you 'd find any babies here!" exclaimed the Dream Fairies. "Why, in all this bright light the babies would never, never go to sleep! Oh, no; we 'll have to look for the babies on the other side of the Moon."

"Of course we shall," said Sweet One Darling. "I might have guessed as much if I 'd only stopped to think."

The Dream Fairies showed Sweet One Darling how to get to the edge of the Moon, and when she had crawled there she held on to the edge very fast and peeped over as cautiously as if she had been a timid little mouse instead of the bravest Sweet One Darling in all the world. She was very cautious and quiet, because the Dream Fairies had told her that she must be very sure not to awaken any of the little babies, for there are no Mothers up there on the other side of the Moon, and if by any chance a little baby is awakened why, as you would easily suppose, the consequences are exceedingly embarrassing.

"Can you see anything?" asked the Dream Fairies of Sweet One Darling as she clung to the edge of the Moon and peeped over.

"I should say I did!" exclaimed Sweet One Darling. "I never supposed there could be so beautiful a place. I see a large, fair garden, filled with shrubbery and flowers; there are fountains and velvety hillocks and silver lakes and embowered nooks. A soft, dim, golden light broods over the quiet spot."

"Yes, that is the light which shines through the Moon from the bright side; but it is very faint," said the Dream Fairies.

"And I see the little babies asleep," continued Sweet One Darling. "They are lying in the embowered nooks, near the fountains, upon the velvety hillocks, amid the flowers, under the trees, and upon the broad leaves of the lilies in the silver lakes. How cunning and plump and sweet they are I must take some of them back with me!"

If they had not been afraid of waking the babies the Dream Fairies would have laughed uproariously at this suggestion. Just fancy Sweet One Darling, a baby herself, undertaking the care of a lot of other little babies fresh from the garden on the other side of the Moon!

"I wonder how they all came here in this Moon Garden?" asked Sweet One Darling. And the Dream Fairies told her.

They explained that whenever a mother upon earth asked for a little baby of her own her prayer floated up and up many leagues up and was borne to the other side of the Moon, where it fell and rested upon a lily leaf or upon a bank of flowers in that beautiful garden. And resting there the prayer presently grew and grew until it became a cunning little baby! So when the Doctor Man came with his box the baby was awaiting him, and he had only to carry the precious little thing to the Mother and give her prayer back to her to keep and to love always. There are so very many of these tiny babies in the Moon Garden that sometimes he does n't do it of purpose but sometimes the Doctor Man brings the baby to the wrong mother, and that makes the real mother, who prayed for the baby, feel very, very badly.

Well, I actually believe that Sweet One Darling would gladly have spent the rest of her life clinging to the edge of the Moon and peeping over at the babies in that beautiful garden. But the Dream Fairies agreed that this would never do at all. They finally got Sweet One Darling away by promising to stop on their journey home to replenish her nursing bottle at the Milky Way, which, as perhaps you know, is a marvellous lacteal ocean in the very midst of the sky. This beverage had so peculiar and so soothing a charm that presently Sweet One Darling went sound asleep, and when she woke up goodness me! it was late in the morning, and her brother, little Our Golden Son, was standing by her cradle, wondering why she did n't wake up to look at his beautiful new toy elephant.

Sweet One Darling told Good Old Soul and little Our Golden Son all about the garden on the other side of the Moon.

"I am sure it is true," said Good Old Soul. "And now that I come to think of it, that is the reason why the Moon always turns her bright side toward our earth! If the other side were turned this way the light of the sun and the noise we make would surely awaken and frighten those poor little babies!"

Little Our Golden Son believed the story, too. And if Good Old Soul and little Our Golden Son believed it, why should n't you? If it were not true how could I have known all about it and told it to you?

SAMUEL COWLES AND HIS HORSE ROYAL

The day on which I was twelve years old my father said to me: "Samuel, walk down the lane with me to the pasture lot; I want to show you something." Never suspicioning anything, I trudged along with father, and what should I find in the pasture lot but the cunningest, prettiest, liveliest colt a boy ever clapped eyes on!

"That is my birthday present to you," said father. "Yes, Samuel, I give the colt to you to do with as you like, for you 've been a good boy and have done well at school."

You can easily understand that my boyish heart overflowed with pride and joy and gratitude. A great many years have elapsed since that time, but I have n't forgotten and I never shall forget the delight of that moment, when I realized that I had a colt of my own a real, live colt, and a Morgan colt, at that!

"How old is he, father?" I asked.

"A week old, come to morrow," said father.

"Has Judge Phipps seen him yet?" I asked.

"No; nobody has seen him but you and me and the hired man."

Judge Phipps was the justice of the peace. I had a profound respect for him, for what he did n't know about horses was n't worth knowing; I was sure of this, because the judge himself told me so. One of the first duties to which I applied myself was to go and get the judge and show him the colt. The judge praised the pretty creature inordinately, enumerating all his admirable points and predicting a famous career for him. The judge even went so far as to express the conviction that in due time my colt would win "imperishable renown and immortal laurels as a competitor at the meetings of the Hampshire County Trotting Association," of which association the judge was the president, much to the scandal of his estimable wife, who viewed with pious horror her husband's connection with the race track.

"What do you think I ought to name my colt?" I asked of the judge.

"When I was about your age," the judge answered, "I had a colt and I named him Royal. He won all the premiums at the county fair before he was six year old."

That was quite enough for me. To my thinking every utterance of the judge's was ex cathedra; moreover, in my boyish exuberance, I fancied that this name would start my colt auspiciously upon a famous career; I began at once to think and to speak of him as the prospective winner of countless honors.

From the moment when I first set eyes on Royal I was his stanch friend; even now, after the lapse of years, I cannot think of my old companion without feeling here in my breast a sense of gratitude that that honest, patient, loyal friend entered so largely into my earlier life.

Twice a day I used to trudge down the lane to the pasture lot to look at the colt, and invariably I was accompanied by a troop of boy acquaintants who heartily envied me my good luck, and who regaled me constantly with suggestions of what they would do if Royal were their colt. Royal soon became friendly with us all, and he would respond to my call, whinnying to me as I came down the lane, as much as to say: "Good morning to you, little master! I hope you are coming to have a romp with me." And, gracious! how he would curve his tail and throw up his head and gather his short body together and trot around the pasture lot on those long legs of his! He enjoyed life, Royal did, as much as we boys enjoyed it.

Naturally enough, I made all sorts of plans for Royal. I recall that, after I had been on a visit to Springfield and had beholden for the first time the marvels of Barnum's show, I made up my mind that when Royal and I were old enough we would unite our fortunes with those of a circus, and in my imagination I already pictured huge and gaudy posters announcing the blood curdling performances of the dashing bareback equestrian, Samuel Cowles, upon his fiery Morgan steed, Royal! This plan was not at all approved of by Judge Phipps, who continued to insist that it was on the turf and not in the sawdust circle that Royal's genius lay, and to this way of thinking I was finally converted, but not until the judge had promised to give me a sulky as soon as Royal demonstrated his ability to make a mile in 2:40.

It is not without a sigh of regret that in my present narrative I pass over the five years next succeeding the date of Royal's arrival. For they were very happy years indeed, at this distant period I am able to recall only that my boyhood was full, brimful of happiness. I broke Royal myself; father and the hired man stood around and made suggestions, and at times they presumed to take a hand in the proceedings. Virtually, however, I broke Royal to the harness and to the saddle, and after that I was even more attached to him than ever before you know how it is, if ever you 've broken a colt yourself!

When I went away to college it seemed to me that leaving Royal was almost as hard as leaving mother and father; you see the colt had become a very large part of my boyish life followed me like a pet dog, was lonesome when I was n't round, used to rub his nose against my arm and look lovingly at me out of his big, dark, mournful eyes yes, I cried when I said good by to him the morning I started for Williamstown. I was ashamed of it then, but not now no, not now.

But my fun was all the keener, I guess, when I came home at vacation times. Then we had it, up hill and down dale Royal and I did! In the summer time along the narrow roads we trailed, and through leafy lanes, and in my exultation I would cut at the tall weeds at the roadside and whisk at the boughs arching overhead, as if I were a warrior mounted for battle and these other things were human victims to my valor. In the winter we sped away over the snow and ice, careless to the howling of the wind and the wrath of the storm. Royal knew the favorite road, every inch of the way; he knew, too, when Susie held the reins Susie was Judge Phipps' niece, and I guess she 'd have mittened me if it had n't been that I had the finest colt in the county!

The summer I left college there came to me an overwhelming sense of patriotic duty. Mother was the first to notice my absent mindedness, and to her I first confided the great wish of my early manhood. It is hard for parents to bid a son go forth to do service upon the battlefield, but New England in those times responded cheerfully and nobly to Mr. Lincoln's call. The Eighth Massachusetts cavalry was the regiment I enlisted in; a baker's dozen of us boys went together from the quiet little village nestling in the shadow of Mount Holyoke. From Camp Andrew I wrote back a piteous letter, complaining of the horse that had been assigned to me; I wanted Royal; we had been inseparable in times of peace why should we not share together the fortunes of war? Within a fortnight along came Royal, conducted in all dignity by you would never guess by Judge Phipps! Full of patriotism and of cheer was the judge.

"Both of ye are thoroughbreds," said he. "Ye 'll come in under the wire first every time, I know ye will."

The judge also brought me a saddle blanket which Susie had ornamented with wondrous and tender art.

So Royal and I went into the war together. There were times of privation and of danger; neither of us ever complained. I am proud to bear witness that in every emergency my horse bore himself with a patience and a valor that seemed actually human. My comrades envied me my gentle, stanch, obedient servant. Indeed, Royal and I became famous as inseparable and loyal friends.

We were in five battles and neither of us got even so much as a scratch. But one afternoon in a skirmish with the rebels near Potomac Mills a bullet struck me in the thigh, and from the mere shock I fell from Royal's back into the tangle of the thicket. The fall must have stunned me, for the next thing I knew I was alone deserted of all except my faithful horse. Royal stood over me, and when I opened my eyes he gave a faint whinny. I hardly knew what to do. My leg pained me excruciatingly. I surmised that I would never be able to make my way back to camp under the fire of the rebel picketers, for I discovered that they were closing in.

Then it occurred to me to pin a note to Royal's saddle blanket and to send Royal back to camp telling the boys of the trouble I was in. The horse understood it all; off he galloped, conscious of the import of the mission upon which he had been dispatched. Bang bang bang! went the guns over yonder, as if the revengeful creatures in the far off brush guessed the meaning of our manoeuvering and sought to slay my loyal friend. But not a bullet touched him leastwise he galloped on and on till I lost sight of him. They came for me at last, the boys did; they were a formidable detachment, and how the earth shook as they swept along!

"We thought you were a goner, sure," said Hi Bixby.

"I guess I would have been if it had n't been for Royal," said I.

"I guess so, myself," said he. "When we saw him stumblin' along all bloody we allowed for sure you was dead!"

"All blood?" I cried. "Is Royal hurt?"

"As bad as a hoss can be," said he.

In camp we found them doing the best they could for him. But it was clearly of no avail. There was a gaping, ragged hole in his side; seeking succor for me, Royal had met his death wound. I forgot my own hurt; I thrust the others aside and hobbled where he lay.

"Poor old Roy!" I cried, as I threw myself beside my dying friend and put my arms about his neck. Then I patted and stroked him and called him again and again by name, and there was a look in his eyes that told me he knew me and was glad that I was there.

How strange, and yet how beautiful, it was that in that far off country, with my brave, patient, loyal friend's fluttering heart close unto mine, I neither saw nor thought of the scene around me.

But before my eyes came back the old, familiar places the pasture lot, the lane, the narrow road up the hill, the river winding along between great stretches of brown corn, the aisle of maple trees, and the fountain where we drank so many, many times together and I smelled the fragrance of the flowers and trees abloom, and I heard the dear voices and the sweet sounds of my boyhood days.

Then presently a mighty shudder awakened me from this dreaming. And I cried out with affright and grief, for I felt that I was alone.

THE WEREWOLF

In the reign of Egbert the Saxon there dwelt in Britain a maiden named Yseult, who was beloved of all, both for her goodness and for her beauty. But, though many a youth came wooing her, she loved Harold only, and to him she plighted her troth.

Among the other youth of whom Yseult was beloved was Alfred, and he was sore angered that Yseult showed favor to Harold, so that one day Alfred said to Harold: "Is it right that old Siegfried should come from his grave and have Yseult to wife?" Then added he, "Prithee, good sir, why do you turn so white when I speak your grandsire's name?"

Then Harold asked, "What know you of Siegfried that you taunt me? What memory of him should vex me now?"

"We know and we know," retorted Alfred. "There are some tales told us by our grandmas we have not forgot."

So ever after that Alfred's words and Alfred's bitter smile haunted Harold by day and night.

Harold's grandsire, Siegfried the Teuton, had been a man of cruel violence. The legend said that a curse rested upon him, and that at certain times he was possessed of an evil spirit that wreaked its fury on mankind. But Siegfried had been dead full many years, and there was naught to mind the world of him save the legend and a cunning wrought spear which he had from Brunehilde, the witch. This spear was such a weapon that it never lost its brightness, nor had its point been blunted. It hung in Harold's chamber, and it was the marvel among weapons of that time.

Yseult knew that Alfred loved her, but she did not know of the bitter words which Alfred had spoken to Harold. Her love for Harold was perfect in its trust and gentleness. But Alfred had hit the truth: the curse of old Siegfried was upon Harold slumbering a century, it had awakened in the blood of the grandson, and Harold knew the curse that was upon him, and it was this that seemed to stand between him and Yseult. But love is stronger than all else, and Harold loved.

Harold did not tell Yseult of the curse that was upon him, for he feared that she would not love him if she knew. Whensoever he felt the fire of the curse burning in his veins he would say to her, "To morrow I hunt the wild boar in the uttermost forest," or, "Next week I go stag stalking among the distant northern hills." Even so it was that he ever made good excuse for his absence, and Yseult thought no evil things, for she was trustful; ay, though he went many times away and was long gone, Yseult suspected no wrong. So none beheld Harold when the curse was upon him in its violence.

Alfred alone bethought himself of evil things. "'T is passing strange," quoth he, "that ever and anon this gallant lover should quit our company and betake himself whither none knoweth. In sooth 't will be well to have an eye on old Siegfried's grandson."

Harold knew that Alfred watched him zealously, and he was tormented by a constant fear that Alfred would discover the curse that was on him; but what gave him greater anguish was the fear that mayhap at some moment when he was in Yseult's presence, the curse would seize upon him and cause him to do great evil unto her, whereby she would be destroyed or her love for him would be undone forever. So Harold lived in terror, feeling that his love was hopeless, yet knowing not how to combat it.

Now, it befell in those times that the country round about was ravaged of a werewolf, a creature that was feared by all men howe'er so valorous. This werewolf was by day a man, but by night a wolf given to ravage and to slaughter, and having a charmed life against which no human agency availed aught. Wheresoever he went he attacked and devoured mankind, spreading terror and desolation round about, and the dream readers said that the earth would not be freed from the werewolf until some man offered himself a voluntary sacrifice to the monster's rage.

Now, although Harold was known far and wide as a mighty huntsman, he had never set forth to hunt the werewolf, and, strange enow, the werewolf never ravaged the domain while Harold was therein. Whereat Alfred marvelled much, and oftentimes he said: "Our Harold is a wondrous huntsman. Who is like unto him in stalking the timid doe and in crippling the fleeing boar? But how passing well doth he time his absence from the haunts of the werewolf. Such valor beseemeth our young Siegfried."

Which being brought to Harold his heart flamed with anger, but he made no answer, lest he should betray the truth he feared.

It happened so about that time that Yseult said to Harold, "Wilt thou go with me to morrow even to the feast in the sacred grove?"

"That can I not do," answered Harold. "I am privily summoned hence to Normandy upon a mission of which I shall some time tell thee. And I pray thee, on thy love for me, go not to the feast in the sacred grove without me."

"What say'st thou?" cried Yseult. "Shall I not go to the feast of Ste. Aelfreda? My father would be sore displeased were I not there with the other maidens. 'T were greatest pity that I should despite his love thus."

"But do not, I beseech thee," Harold implored. "Go not to the feast of Ste. Aelfreda in the sacred grove! And thou would thus love me, go not see, thou my life, on my two knees I ask it!"

"How pale thou art," said Yseult, "and trembling."

"Go not to the sacred grove upon the morrow night," he begged.

Yseult marvelled at his acts and at his speech. Then, for the first time, she thought him to be jealous whereat she secretly rejoiced (being a woman).

"Ah," quoth she, "thou dost doubt my love," but when she saw a look of pain come on his face she added as if she repented of the words she had spoken "or dost thou fear the werewolf?"

Then Harold answered, fixing his eyes on hers, "Thou hast said it; it is the werewolf that I fear."

"Why dost thou look at me so strangely, Harold?" cried Yseult. "By the cruel light in thine eyes one might almost take thee to be the werewolf!"

"Come hither, sit beside me," said Harold tremblingly, "and I will tell thee why I fear to have thee go to the feast of Ste. Aelfreda to morrow evening. Hear what I dreamed last night. I dreamed I was the werewolf do not shudder, dear love, for 't was only a dream.

"A grizzled old man stood at my bedside and strove to pluck my soul from my bosom.

"'What would'st thou?' I cried.

"'Thy soul is mine,' he said, 'thou shalt live out my curse. Give me thy soul hold back thy hands give me thy soul, I say.'

"'Thy curse shall not be upon me,' I cried. 'What have I done that thy curse should rest upon me? Thou shalt not have my soul.'

"'For my offence shalt thou suffer, and in my curse thou shalt endure hell it is so decreed.'

"So spake the old man, and he strove with me, and he prevailed against me, and he plucked my soul from my bosom, and he said, 'Go, search and kill' and and lo, I was a wolf upon the moor.

"The dry grass crackled beneath my tread. The darkness of the night was heavy and it oppressed me. Strange horrors tortured my soul, and it groaned and groaned, gaoled in that wolfish body. The wind whispered to me; with its myriad voices it spake to me and said, 'Go, search and kill.' And above these voices sounded the hideous laughter of an old man. I fled the moor whither I knew not, nor knew I what motive lashed me on.

"I came to a river and I plunged in. A burning thirst consumed me, and I lapped the waters of the river they were waves of flame, and they flashed around me and hissed, and what they said was, 'Go, search and kill,' and I heard the old man's laughter again.

"A forest lay before me with its gloomy thickets and its sombre shadows with its ravens, its vampires, its serpents, its reptiles, and all its hideous brood of night. I darted among its thorns and crouched amid the leaves, the nettles, and the brambles. The owls hooted at me and the thorns pierced my flesh. 'Go, search and kill,' said everything. The hares sprang from my pathway; the other beasts ran bellowing away; every form of life shrieked in my ears the curse was on me I was the werewolf.

"On, on I went with the fleetness of the wind, and my soul groaned in its wolfish prison, and the winds and the waters and the trees bade me, 'Go, search and kill, thou accursed brute; go, search and kill.'

"Nowhere was there pity for the wolf; what mercy, thus, should I, the werewolf, show? The curse was on me and it filled me with a hunger and a thirst for blood. Skulking on my way within myself I cried, 'Let me have blood, oh, let me have human blood, that this wrath may be appeased, that this curse may be removed.'

"At last I came to the sacred grove. Sombre loomed the poplars, the oaks frowned upon me. Before me stood an old man 'twas he, grizzled and taunting, whose curse I bore. He feared me not. All other living things fled before me, but the old man feared me not. A maiden stood beside him. She did not see me, for she was blind.

"Kill, kill,' cried the old man, and he pointed at the girl beside him.

"Hell raged within me the curse impelled me I sprang at her throat. I heard the old man's laughter once more, and then then I awoke, trembling, cold, horrified."

Scarce was this dream told when Alfred strode that way.

"Now, by'r Lady," quoth he, "I bethink me never to have seen a sorrier twain."

Then Yseult told him of Harold's going away and how that Harold had besought her not to venture to the feast of Ste. Aelfreda in the sacred grove.

"These fears are childish," cried Alfred boastfully. "And thou sufferest me, sweet lady, I will bear thee company to the feast, and a score of my lusty yeomen with their good yew bows and honest spears, they shall attend me. There be no werewolf, I trow, will chance about with us."

Whereat Yseult laughed merrily, and Harold said: "'T is well; thou shalt go to the sacred grove, and may my love and Heaven's grace forefend all evil."

Then Harold went to his abode, and he fetched old Siegfried's spear back unto Yseult, and he gave it into her two hands, saying, "Take this spear with thee to the feast to morrow night. It is old Siegfried's spear, possessing mighty virtue and marvellous."

And Harold took Yseult to his heart and blessed her, and he kissed her upon her brow and upon her lips, saying, "Farewell, oh, my beloved. How wilt thou love me when thou know'st my sacrifice. Farewell, farewell forever, oh, alder liefest mine."

So Harold went his way, and Yseult was lost in wonderment.

On the morrow night came Yseult to the sacred grove wherein the feast was spread, and she bore old Siegfried's spear with her in her girdle. Alfred attended her, and a score of lusty yeomen were with him. In the grove there was great merriment, and with singing and dancing and games withal did the honest folk celebrate the feast of the fair Ste. Aelfreda.

But suddenly a mighty tumult arose, and there were cries of "The werewolf!" "The werewolf!" Terror seized upon all stout hearts were frozen with fear. Out from the further forest rushed the werewolf, wood wroth, bellowing hoarsely, gnashing his fangs and tossing hither and thither the yellow foam from his snapping jaws. He sought Yseult straight, as if an evil power drew him to the spot where she stood. But Yseult was not afeared; like a marble statue she stood and saw the werewolf's coming. The yeomen, dropping their torches and casting aside their bows, had fled; Alfred alone abided there to do the monster battle.

At the approaching wolf he hurled his heavy lance, but as it struck the werewolf's bristling back the weapon was all to shivered.

Then the werewolf, fixing his eyes upon Yseult, skulked for a moment in the shadow of the yews and thinking then of Harold's words, Yseult plucked old Siegfried's spear from her girdle, raised it on high, and with the strength of despair sent it hurtling through the air.

The werewolf saw the shining weapon, and a cry burst from his gaping throat a cry of human agony. And Yseult saw in the werewolf's eyes the eyes of some one she had seen and known, but 't was for an instant only, and then the eyes were no longer human, but wolfish in their ferocity. A supernatural force seemed to speed the spear in its flight. With fearful precision the weapon smote home and buried itself by half its length in the werewolf's shaggy breast just above the heart, and then, with a monstrous sigh as if he yielded up his life without regret the werewolf fell dead in the shadow of the yews.

Then, ah, then in very truth there was great joy, and loud were the acclaims, while, beautiful in her trembling pallor, Yseult was led unto her home, where the people set about to give great feast to do her homage, for the werewolf was dead, and she it was that had slain him.

But Yseult cried out: "Go, search for Harold go, bring him to me. Nor eat, nor sleep till he be found."

"Good my lady," quoth Alfred, "how can that be, since he hath betaken himself to Normandy?"

"I care not where he be," she cried. "My heart stands still until I look into his eyes again."

"Surely he hath not gone to Normandy," outspake Hubert. "This very eventide I saw him enter his abode."

They hastened thither a vast company. His chamber door was barred.

"Harold, Harold, come forth!" they cried, as they beat upon the door, but no answer came to their calls and knockings. Afeared, they battered down the door, and when it fell they saw that Harold lay upon his bed.

"He sleeps," said one. "See, he holds a portrait in his hand and it is her portrait. How fair he is and how tranquilly he sleeps."

But no, Harold was not asleep. His face was calm and beautiful, as if he dreamed of his beloved, but his raiment was red with the blood that streamed from a wound in his breast a gaping, ghastly spear wound just above his heart.

A MARVELLOUS INVENTION

It is narrated, that, once upon a time, there lived a youth who required so much money for the gratification of his dissolute desires, that he was compelled to sell his library in order to secure funds. Thereupon, he despatched a letter to his venerable father, saying, "Rejoice with me, O father! for already am I beginning to live upon the profits of my books."

Professor Andrew J. Thorpe has invented an ingenious machine which will be likely to redound to the physical comfort and the intellectual benefit of our fellow citizens. We are disposed to treat of this invention at length, for two reasons: first, because it is a Chicago invention; and, second, because it seems particularly calculated to answer an important demand that has existed in Chicago for a long time. Professor Thorpe's machine is nothing less than a combination parlor, library, and folding bedstead, adapted to the drawing room, the study, the dining room, and the sleeping apartment a producer capable of giving to the world thousands upon thousands of tomes annually, and these, too, in a shape most attractive to our public.

Professor Thorpe himself is of New England birth and education; and, until became West, he was called "Uncle Andy Thorpe." For many years he lived in New Britain, Connecticut; and there he pursued the vocation of a manufacturer of sofas, settees, settles, and bed lounges. He came to Chicago three years ago; and not long thereafter, he discovered that the most imperative demand of this community was for a bed which combined, "at one and the same time" (as he says, for he is no rhetorician), the advantages of a bed and the advantages of a library. In a word, Chicago was a literary centre; and it required, even in the matter of its sleeping apparata, machines which, when not in use for bed purposes, could be utilized to the nobler ends of literary display.

In this emergency the fertile Yankee wit of the immigrant came to his assistance; and about a year ago he put upon the market the ingenious and valuable combination which has commanded the admiration and patronage of our best literary circles, and which at this moment we are pleased to discourse of.

It has been our good fortune to inspect the superb line of folding library bedsteads which Professor Thorpe offers to the public at startlingly low figures, and we are surprised at the ingenuity and the learning apparent in these contrivances. The Essay bedstead is a particularly handsome piece of furniture, being made of polished mahogany, elaborately carved, and intricately embellished throughout. When closed, this bedstead presents the verisimilitude of a large book case filled with the essays of Emerson, Carlyle, Bacon, Montaigne, Hume, Macaulay, Addison, Steele, Johnson, Budgell, Hughes, and others. These volumes are made in one piece, of the best seasoned oak, and are hollow within throughout; so that each shelf constitutes in reality a chest or drawer which may be utilized for divers domestic purposes. In these drawers a husband may keep his shirts or neckties; or in them a wife may stow away her furs or flannel underwear in summer, and her white piques and muslins in winter.

These drawers (each of which extends to the height of twelve inches) are faced in superb tree calf, and afford a perfect representation of rows of books, the title and number of each volume being printed in massive gold characters. The weight of the six drawers in this Essay bedstead does not exceed twelve pounds; but the machine is so stoutly built as to admit of the drawers containing a weight equivalent to six hundred pounds without interfering with the ease and nicety of the machine's operation. Upon touching a gold mounted knob, the book case divides, the front part of it descends; and, presto! you have as beautiful a couch as ever Sancho could have envied.

This Essay bedstead is sold for four hundred and fifty dollars. Another design, with the case and bed in black walnut, the books in papier maché, and none but English essayists in the Collection, can be had for a hundred dollars.

A British Poets' folding bed can be had for three hundred dollars. This is an imitation of the blue and gold edition published in Boston some years ago. Busts of Shakespeare and of Wordsworth appear at the front upper corners of the book case, and these serve as pedestals to the machine when it is unfolded into a bedstead. This style, we are told by Professor Thorpe, has been officially indorsed by the poetry committee of the Chicago Literary Club. A second design, in royal octavo white pine, and omitting the works of Chaucer, Spenser, Ben Jonson, and Herrick, is quoted at a hundred and fifty dollars.

The Historical folding bed contains complete sets of Hume, Gibbon, Guizot, Prescott, Macaulay, Bancroft, Lingard, Buckle, etc., together with Haines's "History of Lake County Indians" and Peck's "Gazetteer of Illinois," bound in half calf, and having a storage space of three feet by fourteen inches to each row, there being six rows of these books. You can get this folding bed for two hundred dollars, or there is a second set in cloth that can be had for a hundred dollars.

The Dramatists' folding bed (No. 1) costs three hundred dollars, bound in tree calf hard maple, the case being in polished cherry, elaborately carved. The works included in this library are Shakespeare's, Schiller's, Molière's, Goethe's, Jonson's, Bartley Campbell's, and many others. Style No. 2 of this folding bed has not yet been issued, owing to some difficulty which Professor Thorpe has had with eastern publishers; but when the matter of copyright has been adjusted, the works of Plautus, Euripides, Thucydides, and other classic dramatists will be brought out for the delectation of appreciative Chicagoans.

The Novelists' bed can be had in numerous styles. One contains the novels of Mackenzie, Fielding, Smollett, Walpole, Dickens, Thackeray, and Scott, and is bound in tree calf: another, better adapted to the serious minded (especially to young women), is made up of the novels of Maria Edgeworth, Miss Jane Porter, Miss Burney, and the Rev. E. P. Roe. This style can be had for fifty dollars. But the Novelists' folding bed is manufactured in a dozen different styles, and one should consult the catalogue before ordering.

THE STORY OF XANTHIPPE

CHICAGO, ILL.

TO THE EDITOR: I am in a great dilemma, and I come to you for counsel. I love and wish to marry a young carpenter who has been waiting on me for two years. My father wants me to marry a literary man fifteen years older than myself, a very smart man I will admit, but I fancy he is too smart for me. I much prefer the young carpenter, yet father says a marriage with the literary man would give me the social position he fancies I would enjoy. Now, what am I to do? What would you do, if you were I?

Yours in trouble, PRISCILLA.

Listen, gentle maiden, and ye others of her sex, to the story of Xanthippe, the Athenian woman.

Very, very many years ago there dwelt in Athens a fruit dealer of the name of Kimon, who was possessed of two daughters, the one named Helen and the other Xanthippe. At the age of twenty, Helen was wed to Aristagoras the tinker, and went with him to abide in his humble dwelling in the suburbs of Athens, about one parasang's distance from the Acropolis.

Xanthippe, the younger sister, gave promise of singular beauty; and at an early age she developed a wit that was the marvel and the joy of her father's household, and of the society that was to be met with there. Prosperous in a worldly way, Kimon was enabled to give this favorite daughter the best educational advantages; and he was justly proud when at the age of nineteen Xanthippe was graduated from the Minerva Female College with all the highest honors of her class. There was but one thing that cast a shadow upon the old gentleman's happiness, and that was his pain at observing that among all Xanthippe's associates there was one upon whom she bestowed her sweetest smiles; namely, Gatippus, the son of Heliopharnes the plasterer.

"My daughter," said Kimon, "you are now of an age when it becomes a maiden to contemplate marriage as a serious and solemn probability: therefore I beseech you to practise the severest discrimination in the choice of your male associates, and I enjoin upon you to have naught to say or to do with any youth that might not be considered an eligible husband; for, by the dog! it is my wish to see you wed to one of good station."

Kimon thereupon proceeded to tell his daughter that his dearest ambition had been a desire to unite her in marriage with a literary man. He saw that the tendency of the times was in the direction of literature; schools of philosophy were springing up on every side, logic and poetry were prated in every household. Why should not the beautiful and accomplished daughter of Kimon the fruiterer become one of that group of geniuses who were contributing at that particular time to the glory of Athens as the literary centre of the world? The truth was that, having prospered in his trade, Kimon pined for social recognition; it grieved him that one of his daughters had wed a tinker, and he had registered a vow with Pallas that his other daughter should be given into the arms of a worthier man.

Xanthippe was a dutiful daughter; she had been taught to obey her parents; and although her heart inclined to Gatippus, the son of Heliopharnes the plasterer, she smothered all rebellious emotions, and said she would try to do her father's will. Accordingly, therefore, Kimon introduced into his home one evening a certain young Athenian philosopher, a typical literary Bohemian of that time, one Socrates, a creature of wondrous wisdom and ready wit.

The appearance of this suitor, presumptive if not apparent, did not particularly please Xanthippe. Socrates was an ill favored young man. He was tall, raw boned, and gangling. When he walked, he slouched; and when he sat down, he sprawled like a crab upon its back. His coarse hair rebelled upon his head and chin; and he had a broad, flat nose, that had been broken in two places by the kick of an Assyrian mule. Withal, Socrates talked delightfully; and it is not hard to imagine that Xanthippe's pretty face, plump figure, and vivacious manners served as an inspiration to the young philosopher's wit. So it was not long ere Xanthippe found herself entertaining a profound respect for Socrates.

At all events, Xanthippe, the Athenian beauty, was wed to Socrates the philosopher. Putting all thought of Gatippus, the son of Heliopharnes the plasterer, out of her mind, Xanthippe went to the temple of Aphrodite, and was wed to Socrates. Historians differ as to the details of the affair; but it seems generally agreed that Socrates was late at the ceremony, having been delayed on his way to the temple by one Diogenes, who asked to converse with him on the immortality of the soul. Socrates stopped to talk, and would perhaps have been stopping there still had not Kimon hunted him up, and fetched him to the wedding.

A great wedding it was. A complete report of it was written by one of Socrates' friends, another literary man, named Xenophon. The literary guild, including philosophers by the score, were there in full feather, and Xenophon put himself to the trouble of giving a complete list of these distinguished persons; and to the report, as it was penned for the "Athens Weekly Papyrus," he appended a fine puff of Socrates, which has led posterity to surmise that Socrates conferred a great compliment on Xanthippe in marrying her. Yet, what else could we expect of this man Xenophon? The only other thing he ever did was to conduct a retreat from a Persian battle field.

And now began the trials of Xanthippe, the wife of the literary man. Ay, it was not long ere the young wife discovered that, of all husbands in the world, the literary husband was the hardest to get along with. Always late at his meals, always absorbed in his work, always indifferent to the comforts of home what a trial this man Socrates must have been! Why, half the time, poor Xanthippe did n't know where the next month's rent was coming from; and as for the grocer's and butcher's bills well, between this creditor and that creditor the tormented little wife's life fast became a burden to her. Had it not been for her father's convenient fruit stall, Xanthippe must have starved; and, at best, fruit as a regular diet is hardly preferable to starvation. And while she scrimped and saved, and made her own gowns, and patched up the children's kilts as best she might, Socrates stood around the streets talking about the immortality of the soul and the vanity of human life!

Many times Xanthippe pined for the amusements and seductive gayeties of social life, but she got none. The only society she knew was the prosy men folk whom Socrates used to fetch home with him occasionally. Xanthippe grew to hate them, and we don't blame her. Just imagine that dirty old Diogenes lolling around on the furniture, and expressing his preference for a tub; picking his teeth with his jack knife, and smoking his wretched cob pipe in the parlor!

"Socrates, dear," Xanthippe would say at times, "please take me to the theatre to night; I do so want to see that new tragedy by Euclydides."

But Socrates would swear by Hercules, or by the dog, or by some other classic object, that he had an engagement with the rhetoricians, or with the sophists, or with Alcibiades, or with Crito, or with some of the rest of the boys he called them philosophers, but we know what he meant by that.

So it was toil and disappointment, disappointment and toil, from one month's end to another's; and so the years went by.

Sometimes Xanthippe rebelled; but, with all her wit, how could she reason with Socrates, the most gifted and the wisest of all philosophers? He had a provoking way of practising upon her the exasperating methods of Socratic debate, a system he had invented, and for which he still is revered. Never excited or angry himself, he would ply her with questions until she found herself entangled in a network of contradictions; and then she would be driven, willy nilly, to that last argument of woman "because." Then Socrates the brute! would laugh at her, and would go out and sit on the front door steps, and look henpecked. This is positively the meanest thing a man can do!

"Look at that poor man," said the wife of Edippus the cobbler. "I do believe his wife is cruel to him: see how sad and lonesome he is."

"Don't play with those Socrates children," said another matron. "Their mother must be a dreadful shiftless creature to let her young ones run the streets in such patched up clothes."

So up and down the street the neighbors gossiped oh! it was very humiliating to Xanthippe.

Meanwhile Helen lived in peace with Aristagoras the tinker. Their little home was cosey and comfortable. Xanthippe used to go to see them sometimes, but the sight of their unpretentious happiness made her even more miserable. Meanwhile, too, Xanthippe's old beau, Gatippus, had married; and from Thessaly came reports of the beautiful vineyard and the many wine presses he had acquired. So Xanthippe's life became somewhat more than a struggle; it became a martyrdom. And the wrinkles came into Xanthippe's face, and Xanthippe's hair grew gray, and Xanthippe's heart was filled with the bitterness of disappointment. And the years, full of grind and of poverty and of neglect, crept wearily on.

Time is the grim old collector who goes dunning for the abused wife, and Time finally forced a settlement with Socrates.

Having loafed around Athens for many years to the neglect of his family, and having obtruded his views touching the immortality of the soul upon certain folk who believed that the first duty of a man was to keep his family from starving to death, Socrates was apprehended on a bench warrant, thrown into jail, tried by a jury, and sentenced to die.

It was in this emergency that the great, the divine nobility of the wife asserted itself. She had been neglected by this man, she had gone in rags for him, she had sacrificed her beauty and her hopes and her pride, she had endured the pity of her neighbors, she had heard her children cry with hunger ay, all for him; yet, when a righteous fate o'ertook him, she forgot all the misery of his doing, and she went to him to be his comforter.

Well, she could not have done otherwise, for she was a woman.

Where was his philosophy now? where his wisdom, his logic, his wit? What had become of his disputatious and learned associates that not one of them stood up to plead for the life of Socrates now? Why, the first breath of adversity had blown them away as though they were but mist; and, with these false friends scattered like the coward chaff they were, grim old Socrates turned to Xanthippe for consolation.

She burdened his ears with no reproaches, she spoke not of herself. Her thoughts were of him only, and it was to his chilled spirit that she alone ministered. Not even the horrors of the hemlock draught could drive her from his side, or unloose her arms from about his neck; and when at last the philosopher lay stiff in death, it was Xanthippe that bore away his corpse, and, with spices moistened by her tears, made it ready for the grave.

BAKED BEANS AND CULTURE

The members of the Boston Commercial Club are charming gentlemen. They are now the guests of the Chicago Commercial Club, and are being shown every attention that our market affords. They are a fine looking lot, well dressed and well mannered, with just enough whiskers to be impressive without being imposing.

"This is a darned likely village," said Seth Adams last evening. "Everybody is rushin' 'round an' doin' business as if his life depended on it. Should think they 'd git all tuckered out 'fore night, but I 'll be darned if there ain't just as many folks on the street after nightfall as afore. We 're stoppin' at the Palmer tavern; an' my chamber is up so all fired high that I can count all your meetin' house steeples from the winder."

Last night five or six of these Boston merchants sat around the office of the hotel, and discussed matters and things. Pretty soon they got to talking about beans; this was the subject which they dwelt on with evident pleasure.

"Waal, sir," said Ephraim Taft, a wholesale dealer in maple sugar and flavored lozenges, "you kin talk 'bout your new fashioned dishes an' high falutin vittles; but, when you come right down to it, there ain't no better eatin' than a dish o' baked pork 'n' beans."

"That's so, b'gosh!" chorused the others.

"The truth o' the matter is," continued Mr. Taft, "that beans is good for everybody, 't don't make no difference whether he 's well or sick. Why, I 've known a thousand folks waal, mebbe not quite a thousand; but, waal, now, jest to show, take the case of Bill Holbrook; you remember Bill, don't ye?"

"Bill Holbrook?" said Mr. Ezra Eastman; "why, of course I do! Used to live down to Brimfield, next to the Moses Howard farm."

"That 's the man," resumed Mr. Taft. "Waal, Bill fell sick, kinder moped round, tired like, for a week or two, an' then tuck to his bed. His folks sent for Dock Smith, ol' Dock Smith that used to carry round a pair o' leather saddlebags, gosh, they don't have no sech doctors nowadays! Waal, the dock, he come; an' he looked at Bill's tongue, an' felt uv his pulse, an' said that Bill had typhus fever. Ol' Dock Smith was a very careful, conserv'tive man, an' he never said nothin' unless he knowed he was right.

"Bill began to git wuss, an' he kep' a gittin' wuss every day. One mornin' ol' Dock Smith sez, 'Look a here, Bill, I guess you 're a goner; as I figger it, you can't hol' out till nightfall.'

"Bill's mother insisted on a con sul tation bein' held; so ol' Dock Smith sent over for young Dock Brainerd. I calc'late that, next to ol' Dock Smith, young Dock Brainerd was the smartest doctor that ever lived.

"Waal, pretty soon along come Dock Brainerd; an' he an' Dock Smith went all over Bill, an' looked at his tongue, an felt uv his pulse, an' told him it was a gone case, an' that he had got to die. Then they went off into the spare chamber to hold their con sul tation.

"Waal, Bill he lay there in the front room a pantin' an' a gaspin' an' a wond'rin' whether it wuz true. As he wuz thinkin', up comes the girl to get a clean tablecloth out of the clothes press, an' she left the door ajar as she come in. Bill he gave a sniff, an' his eyes grew more natural like; he gathered together all the strength he had, an' he raised himself up on one elbow, an' sniffed again."

"'Sary,' says he, 'wot's that a cookin'?'

"'Beans,' says she, 'beans for dinner.'

"'Sary,' says the dyin' man, 'I must hev a plate uv them beans!'

"'Sakes alive, Mr. Holbrook!' says she; 'if you wuz to eat any o' them beans, it 'd kill ye!'

"'If I've got to die,'says he, 'I'm goin' to die happy; fetch me a plate uv them beans.'

"Waal, Sary, she pikes off to the doctors.

"'Look a here,' says she. 'Mr. Holbrook smelt the beans cookin', an' he says he 's got to have a plate uv 'em. Now, what shall I do about it?'

"'Waal, doctor,' says Dock Smith, 'what do you think 'bout it?

"'He 's got to die anyhow,' says Dock Brainerd; 'an' I don't suppose the beans 'll make any diff'rence.'

"'That's the way I figger it,' says Dock Smith; 'in all my practice I never knew of beans hurtin' anybody.'

"So Sary went down to the kitchen, an' brought up a plateful of hot baked beans. Dock Smith raised Bill up in bed, an' Dock Brainerd put a piller under the small of Bill's back. Then Sary sat down by the bed, an' fed them beans into Bill until Bill could n't hold any more.

"'How air you feelin' now?' asked Dock Smith.

"Bill did n't say nuthin'; he jest smiled sort uv peaceful like, an' closed his eyes.

"'The end hes come,' said Dock Brainerd sof'ly. 'Bill is dyin'.'

"Then Bill murmured kind o' far away like (as if he was dreamin'), 'I ain't dyin'; I 'm dead an' in heaven.'

"Next mornin' Bill got out uv bed, an' done a big day's work on the farm, an' he hain't hed a sick spell since. Them beans cured him! I tell you, sir, that beans is," etc.

MLLE. PRUD'HOMME'S BOOK

WASHINGTON, D. C., Mai 3.

M. LE REDACTEUR: D'apres votre article dans la "New York Tribune," copie du "Chicago News," je me figure que les habitants de Chicago ayant grand besoin d'un systeme de prononciation francaise, je prends la liberte de vous envoyer par la malle poste le No. 2 d'un ouvrage que je viens de publier; si vous desirez les autres numeros, je me ferai un plaisir de vous les envoyer aussi. Les emballeurs de porc ayant peu de temps a consacrer a l'etude, vu l' omnipotent dollar, seront je crois enchantes et reconnaissants d'un systeme par lequel ils pourront apprendre et comprendre la langue de la fine Sara, au bout de trente lecons, si surtout Monsieur le redacteur veut bien au bout de sa plume spirituelle leur en indiquer le chemin. Sur ce l'auteur du systeme a bien l'honneur de le saluer.

V. PRUD'HOMME.

This is a copy of a pleasant letter we have received from a distinguished Washington lady; we do not print the accentuations, because the Chicago patwor admits of none. A literal rendering of the letter into English is as follows: "From after your article in 'The New York Tribune,' copied from 'The Chicago News,' I to myself have figured that the inhabitants of Chicago having great want of a system of pronunciation French, I take the liberty to you to send by the mail post the number two of a work which I come from to publish; if you desire the other numbers, I to myself will make the pleasure of to you them to send also. The packers of porkers, having little of time to consecrate to the study (owing to the omnipotent dollar), will be, I believe, enchanted and grateful of a system by the which they may learn and understand the language of the clever Sara, at the end of thirty lessons, especially if Mister the editor will at the end of his pen witty to them thereof indicate the road. Whereupon the author of the system has much the honor of him to salute," etc.

We have not given Mdlle. Prud'homme's oovray that conscientious study and that careful research which we shall devote to it just as soon as the tremendous spring rush in local literature eases up a little. The recent opening up of the Straits of Mackinaw, and the prospect of a new railroad line into the very heart of the dialectic region of Indiana, have given Chicago literature so vast an impetus, that we find our review table groaning under the weight of oovrays that demand our scholarly consideration. Mdlle. Prud'homme must understand (for she appears to be exceedingly amiable) that the oovrays of local littérateurs have to be reviewed before the oovrays of outside littérateurs can be taken up. This may seem hard, but it cannot be helped.

Still, we will say that we appreciate, and are grateful for, the uncommon interest which Mdlle. Prud'homme seems to take in the advancement of the French language and French literature in the midst of us. We have heard many of our leading savants and scholiasts frequently express poignant regret that they were unable to read "La Fem de Fu," "Mamzel Zheero Mar Fem," and other noble old French classics whose fame has reached this modern Athens. With the romances of Alexandre Dumas, our public is thoroughly acquainted, having seen the talented James O'Neill in Monty Cristo, and the beautiful and accomplished Grace Hawthorne ("Only an American Girl") in Cameel; yet our more enterprising citizens are keenly aware that there are other French works worthy of perusal intensely interesting works, too, if the steel engravings therein are to be accepted as a criterion.

We doubt not that Mdlle. Prud'homme is desirous of doing Chicago a distinct good; and why, we ask in all seriousness, should this gifted and amiable French scholar not entertain for Chicago somewhat more than a friendly spirit, merely? The first settlers of Chicago were Frenchmen; and, likely as not, some of Mdlle. Prud'homme's ancestors were of the number of those Spartan voyageurs who first sailed down Chicago River, pitched their tents on the spot where Kirk's soap factory now stands, and captured and brought into the refining influences of civilization Long John Wentworth, who at that remote period was frisking about on our prairies, a crude, callow boy, only ten years old, and only seven feet tall.

Chicago was founded by Jeanne Pierre Renaud, one of the original two orphans immortalized by Claxton and Halevy's play in thirteen acts of the same name. At that distant date it was anything but promising; and its prominent industries were Indians, musk rats, and scenery. The only crops harvested were those of malaria, twice per annum, in October and in April, but the yield was sufficient to keep the community well provided all the year round.

THE DEMAND FOR CONDENSED MUSIC

There is a general belief that the mistake made by the managers of the symphony concert in Central Music Hall night before last was in not opening the concert with Beethoven's "Eroica," instead of making it the last number on the programme. We incline to the opinion, however, that, in putting the symphony last, the managers complied with the very first requirement of dramatic composition. This requirement is to the effect that you must not kill all your people off in the first act.

There doubtless are a small number of worthy people who enjoy these old symphonies that are being dragged out of oblivion by glass eyed Teutons from Boston. It may argue a very low grade of intellectuality, spirituality, or whatsoever you may be pleased to call it; but we must confess in all candor, that, much as we revere Mr. Beethoven's memory, we do not fancy having fifty five minute chunks of his musty opi hurled at us.

It is a marvel to us, that, in these progressive times, such leaders as Thomas and Gericke do not respond to the popular demand by providing the public with symphonies in the nutshell. We have condensations in every line except music. Even literature is being boiled down; because in these busy times, people demand a literature which they can read while they run. We have condensed milk, condensed meats, condensed wines, condensed everything but music. What a joyous shout would go up if Thomas or Gericke would only prepare and announce

"SYMPHONIES FOR BUSY PEOPLE! THE OLD MASTERS EPITOMIZED!"

What Chicago demands, and what every enterprising and intelligent community needs, is the highest class of music on the "all the news for two cents" principle. Blanket sheet concertizing must go!

Now, here was this concert, night before last. Two hours and a half to five numbers! Suppose we figure a little on this subject:

EXHIBIT 'A' SYMPHONY.

Total number of minutes	150
Total number of pieces	5
Minutes to each piece	30

EXHIBIT 'B' TRADE.

Total number of minutes	150
Hog slaughtering capacity per minute	3
Total killing	450

Figures will not lie, because (as was the reason with George) they cannot. And figures prove to us, that, in the time consumed by five symphonic numbers, the startling number of four hundred and fifty hogs could be (and are daily) slaughtered, scraped, disembowelled, hewn, and packed. While forty or fifty able bodied musicians are discoursing Beethoven's rambling "Eroica," it were possible to dispatch and to dress a carload of as fine beeves as ever hailed from Texas; and the performance of the "Sakuntala" overture might be regarded as a virtual loss of as much time as would be required for the beheading, skinning, and dismembering of two hundred head of sheep.

These comparisons have probably never occurred to Mr. Thomas or to Mr. Gericke; but they are urged by the patrons of music in Chicago, and therefore they must needs be recognized by the caterers to popular tastes. Chicago society has been founded upon industry, and the culture which she now boasts is conserved only by the strictest attention to business. Nothing is more criminal hereabouts than a waste of time; and it is no wonder, then, that the crème de la crême of our élite lift up their hands, and groan, when they discover that it takes as long to play a classic symphony as it does to slaughter a carload of Missouri razor backs, or an invoice of prairie racers from Kansas.

LEARNING AND LITERATURE

R. J. N. Whiting writes us from New Litchfield, Ill., asking if we can tell him the name of the author of the poem, of which the following is the first stanza:

The weary heart is a pilgrim

Seeking the Mecca of rest;
Its burden is one of sorrows;
And it wails a song as it drags along,
'Tis the song of a hopeless quest.

Mr. Whiting says that this poem has been attributed to James Channahon, a gentleman who flourished about the year 1652; "but," he adds, "its authorship has not as yet been established with any degree of certainty." Mr. Whiting has noticed that the "Daily News" is a "criterion on matters of literary interest," and he craves the boon of our valuable opinion, touching this important question.

Now, although it is true that we occasionally deal with obsolete topics, it is far from our desire to make a practice of so doing. It is natural that, once in a while, when an editor gets hold of a catalogue of unusual merit, and happens to have a line of encyclopaedias at hand it is natural, we say, that, under such circumstances, an editor should take pleasure in letting his subscribers know how learnedly he can write about books and things. But an editor must be careful not to write above the comprehension of the majority of his readers. If we made a practice of writing as learnedly as we are capable of writing, the proprietors of this paper would soon have to raise its price from two cents to five cents per copy.

We say this in no spirit of egotism; it is simply our good fortune that we happen to possess extraordinary advantages. We have the best assortment of cyclopaedias in seven states, and the Public Library is only two blocks off. It is no wonder, therefore, that our erudition and our research are of the highest order.

Still it is not practicable that we, being now on earth, should devote much time to delving into, and wallowing among, the authors of past centuries. Ignatius Donnelly has been trying for the last three years to inveigle us into a discussion as to the authorship of Shakespeare's plays. We have declined to participate in any public brawl with the Minnesota gentleman, for the simple reason that no good could accrue therefrom to anybody. If there were an international copyright law, there would be some use in trying to find out who wrote these plays, in order that the author might claim royalties on his works; or, if not the author, his heirs or assigns forever.

Mr. Whiting will understand that we cannot take much interest in an anonymous hymn of the seventeenth century. It is enough for us to know that the hymn in question could not have been written by a Chicago man, for the very good reason that Chicago did not exist in the seventeenth century; that is to say, it existed merely as the haunt of the musquash and the mud turtle, and not as the living, breathing metropolis of to day. We have our hands full examining into, and criticising, the live topics of current times: if we were to spend our days and nights in hunting up the estray poets and authors of the seventeenth century, how long would it be before the sceptre of trade and culture would slip irrecoverably from Chicago's grasp?

Chicago has very little respect for the seventeenth century, because there is nothing in it. The seventeenth century has done nothing for Chicago: she does not even know that this is the greatest hog market in the world, and she has never had any commercial dealings with us in any line. If Chicago does n't cut a wider swath in history than the seventeenth century has, we shall be very much ashamed of her.

"DIE WALKÜRE" UND DER BOOMERANGELUNGEN

There is a strange fascination about Herr Wagner's musical drama of "Die Walküre." A great many people have supposed that Herr Sullivan's opera of "Das Pinafore" was the most remarkable musical work extant, but we believe the mistake will become apparent as Herr Wagner's masterpiece grows in years.

We will not pretend to say that "Die Walküre" will ever be whistled about the streets, as the airs from "Das Pinafore" are whistled; the fact is, that no rendition of "Die Walküre" can be satisfactory without the accompaniment of weird flashes of fire; and it is hardly to be expected that our youth will carry packages of lycopodium, and boxes of matches, around with them, for the sole purpose of giving the desired effect to any snatches from Herr Wagner's work they may take the notion to whistle. But in the sanctity of our homes, around our firesides, in the front parlor, where the melodeon or the newly hired piano has been set up, it is there that Herr Wagner's name will be revered, and his masterpiece repeated o'er and o'er. The libretto is not above criticism; it strikes us that there is not enough of it. The probability is that Herr Wagner ran out of libretto before he had got through with his music, and therefore had to spread out comparatively few words over a vast expanse of music. The result is that a great part of the time the performers are on the stage is devoted to thought, the orchestra doing a tremendous amount of fiddling, etc., while the actors wander drearily around, with their arms folded across their pulmonary departments, and their minds evidently absorbed in profound cogitation.

As for the music, the only criticism we have to pass upon it is that it changes its subject too often; in this particular it resembles the dictionary, in fact, we believe "Die Walküre" can be termed the Webster's Unabridged of musical language. Herr Wagner has his own way of doing business. He goes at it on the principle of the twelfth man, who holds out against the eleven other jurors, and finally brings them around to his way of thinking.

For instance, in the midst of a pleasing strain in B natural, Herr Wagner has a habit of suddenly bringing out a small reed instrument with a big voice (we do not know its name), piped in the key of F sharp. This small reed instrument will not let go; it holds on to that F sharp like a mortgage. For a brief period the rest of the instruments fiddles, bassoons, viols, flutes, flageolets, cymbals, drums, etc. struggle along with an attempt to either drown the intruder, or bring it around to their way of doing business; but it is vain. Every last one of them has to slide around from B natural to F sharp, and they do it as best they can.

Having accomplished its incendiary and revolutionary purpose, the small reed instrument subsides until it finds another chance to break out. It is a mugwump.

Die Walküren, as given us by the Damrosch Company, are nine stout, comely young women, attired in costumes somewhat similar to the armor worn by Herr Lawrence Barrett's Roman army in Herr Shakespeare's play of "Der Julius Caesar." Readers of Norse mythology may suppose that these weird sisters were dim, vague, shadowy creatures; but they are mistaken. Brunhilde has the embonpoint of a dowager, and her arms are as robust and red as a dairy maid's.

As for Gerhilde, Waltraute, Helmwige, and the rest, they are well fed, buxom ladies, evidently of middle age, whose very appearance exhales an aroma of kraut and garlic, which, by the way, we see by the libretto, was termed "mead" in the days of Wotan and his court. These Die Walküren are said to ride fiery, untamed steeds; but only one steed is exhibited in the drama as it is given at the Columbia. This steed, we regret to say, is a restless, noisy brute, and invariably has to be led off the stage by one of das supes, before his act concludes.

However, no one should doubt his heroic nature, inasmuch as the cabalistic letters "U. S." are distinctly branded upon his left flank.

The Sieglinde of the piece is Fräulein Slach, a young lady no bigger than a minute, but with wonderful powers of endurance. To say nothing of Hunding's persecutions, she has to shield Siegmund, elope with him, climb beetling precipices, ride Brunhilde's fiery, untamed steed, confront die Walküren, and look on her slain lover, and, in addition to these prodigies, participate in a Graeco Roman wrestling match with an orchestra of sixty five pieces for three hours and a half.

Yet she is equal to the emergency. Up to the very last she is as fresh as a daisy; and, after recovering from her swooning spell in the second act, she braces her shoulders back, and dances all around the top notes of the chromatic scale with the greatest of ease. She is a wonderful little woman, is Fräulein Slach! What a wee bit of humanity, yet what a volume of voice she has, and what endurance!

Down among the orchestra people sat a pale, sad man. His apparent lonesomeness interested us deeply. We could not imagine what he was there for. Every once in a while he would get up and leave the orchestra, and dive down under the stage, and appear behind the scenes, where we could catch glimpses of him practising with a pair of thirty pound dumb bells, and testing a spirometer. Then he would come back and re occupy his old seat among the orchestra, and look paler and sadder than ever. What strange, mysterious being was he? Why did he inflict his pale, sad presence upon that galaxy of tuneful revellers?

What a cunning master the great Herr Wagner is! For what emergency does he not provide? It was half past eleven when the third act began. Die Walküren had assembled in the dismal dell, all but the den Walküre, Brunhilde. Wotan is approaching on appalling storm clouds, composed of painted mosquito bars and blue lights. The sheet iron thunder crashes; and the orchestra is engaged in another mortal combat with that revolutionary mugwump, the small reed instrument, that persists in reforming the tune of the opera.

Then the pale, sad man produces a large brass horn, big enough at the business end for a cow to walk into. It is a fearful, ponderous instrument, manufactured especially for "Die Walküre" at the Krupp Gun Factory in Essen. It has an appropriate name: the master himself christened it the boomerangelungen. It is the monarch, the Jumbo of all musical instruments. The cuspidor end of it protrudes into one of the proscenium boxes. The fair occupants of the box are frightened, and timidly shrink back.

Wotan is at hand. He comes upon seven hundred yards of white tarletan, and fourteen pounds of hissing, blazing lycopodium! The pale, sad man at the other end of the boomerangelungen explains his wherefore. He applies his lips to the brazen monster. His eyeballs hang out upon his cheeks, the veins rise on his neck, and the lumpy cords and muscles stand out on his arms and hands. Boohoop, boohoop! yes, six times boohoop does that brazen megatherium blare out, vivid and distinct, above all the other sixty instruments in the orchestra. Then the white tarletan clouds vanish, the blazing lycopodium goes out, and Wotan stands before the excited spectators.

Then the pale, sad man lays down the boomerangelungen, and goes home. That is all he has to do; the six sonorous boohoops, announcing the presence of Wotan, is all that is demanded of the boomerangelungen. But it is enough: it is marvellous, appalling, prodigious.

Whose genius but Herr Wagner's could have found employment for the boomerangelungen? We hear talk of the sword motive, the love motive, the Walhalla motive, and this motive, and that; but they all shrink into nothingness when compared with the motive of the boomerangelungen.

THE WORKS OF SAPPHO

It would be hard to say whether Chicago society is more deeply interested in the circus which is exhibiting on the lake front this week, than in the compilation of Sappho's complete works just published in London, and but this week given to the trade in Chicago. As we understand it, Sappho and the circus had their beginning about the same time: if any thing, the origin of the circus antedated Sappho's birth some years, and has achieved the more wide spread popularity.

In the volume now before us, we learn that Sappho lived in the seventh century before Christ, and that she was at the zenith of her fame at the time when Tarquinius Priscus was king of Rome, and Nebuchadnezzar was subsisting on a hay diet. It appears that, despite her wisdom, this talented lady did not know who her father was; seventeen hundred years after her demise, one Suidas claimed to have discovered that there were seven of her father; but Herodotus gives the name of the gentleman most justly suspected as Scamandronymus. Be this as it may, Sappho married a rich man, and subsequently fell in love with a dude who cared nothing for her; whereupon the unfortunate woman, without waiting to compile her writings, and without even indicating whom she preferred for her literary executor, committed suicide by hurling herself from a high precipice into the sea. Sappho was an exceedingly handsome person, as we see by the engraving which serves as the frontispiece of the work before us. This engraving, as we understand, was made from a portrait painted from life by a contemporaneous old Grecian artist, one Alma Tadema.

Still, we could not help wondering, as we saw the magnificent pageant of Forepaugh's circus sweep down our majestic boulevards and superb thoroughfares yesterday; as we witnessed this imposing spectacle, we say, we could not help wondering how many people in all the vast crowds of spectators knew that there ever was such a poetess as Sappho, or how many, knowing that there was such a party, have ever read her works. It has been nearly a year since a circus came to town; and in that time public taste has been elevated to a degree by theatrical and operatic performers, such as Sara Bernhardt, Emma Abbott, Murray and Murphy, Adele Patti, George C. Miln, Helena Modjeska, Fanny Davenport, and Denman Thompson.

Of course, therefore, our public has come to be able to appreciate with a nicer discrimination and a finer zest the intellectual morceaux and the refined tidbits which Mr. Forepaugh's unparalleled aggregation offers. This was apparent in the vast numbers and in the unbridled enthusiasm of our best citizens gathered upon the housetops and at the street corners along the line of the circus procession. So magnificent a display of silks, satins, and diamonds has seldom been seen: it truly seemed as if the fashion and wealth of our city were trying to vie with the splendors of the glittering circus pageant. In honor of the event, many of the stores, public buildings, and private dwellings displayed banners, mottoes, and congratulatory garlands. From the balcony of the palatial edifice occupied by one of our leading literary clubs was suspended a large banner of pink silk, upon which appeared the word "Welcome" in white; while beneath, upon a scroll, was an appropriate couplet from one of Robert Browning's poems.

When we asked one of the members of this club why the club made such a fuss over the circus, he looked very much astonished; and he answered, "Well, why not? Old Forepaugh is worth over a million dollars, and he always sends us complimentaries whenever he comes to town!"

We asked this same gentleman if he had read the new edition of Sappho's poems. We had a good deal of confidence in his literary judgment and taste, because he is our leading linseed oil dealer; and no man in the West is possessed of more enterprise and sand than he.

"My daughter brought home a copy of the book Saturday," said he, "and I looked through it yesterday. Sappho may suit some cranks; but as for me, give me Ella Wheeler or Will Carleton. I love good poetry: I 've got the finest bound copy of Shakespeare in Illinois, and my edition of Coleridge will knock the socks off any book in the country. My wife has painted all the Doray illustrations of the Ancient Marine, and I would n't swap that book for the costliest Mysonyay in all Paris!

"I can't see where the poetry comes in," he went on to say. "So far as I can make out, this man Sapolio I mean Sappho never did any sustained or consecutive work. His poems read to me a good deal like a diary. Some of them consist of one line only, and quite a number have only three words. Now, I will repeat five entire poems taken from this fool book: I learned them on purpose to repeat at the club. Here is the first,

"Me just now the golden sandalled Dawn.

"That 's all there is to it. Here's the second:

"I yearn and seek.

"A third is complete in

"Much whiter than an egg;

and the fourth is,

"Stir not the shingle,

which, I take it, was one of Sapphire's juvenile poems addressed to his mother. The fifth poem is simply,

"And thou thyself, Calliope,

which, by the way, reminds me that Forepaugh's calliope got smashed up in a railroad accident night before last, a circumstance deeply to be regretted, since there is no instrument calculated to appeal more directly to one versed in mythological lore, or more likely to awaken a train of pleasing associations, than the steam calliope."

A South Side packer, who has the largest library in the city, told us that he had not seen Sappho's works yet, but that he intended to read them at an early date. "I 've got so sick of Howells and James," said he, "that I 'm darned glad to hear that some new fellow has come to the front."

Another prominent social light (a brewer) said that he had bought a "Sappho," and was having it bound in morocco, with turkey red trimmings. "I do enjoy a handsome book," said he. "One of the most valuable volumes in my library I bought of a leading candy manufacturer in this city. It is the original libretto and score of the 'Songs of Solomon,' bound in the tanned pelt of the fatted calf that was killed when the prodigal son came home."

"I have simply glanced through the Sappho book," said another distinguished representative of local culture; "and what surprised me, was the pains that has been taken in getting up the affair. Why, do you know, the editor has gone to the trouble of going through the book, and translating every darned poem into Greek! Of course, this strikes us business men of Chicago as a queer bit of pedantry."

The scholarly and courtly editor of the "Weekly Lard Journal and Literary Companion," Professor A. J. Lyvely, criticised Sappho very freely as he stood at the corner of Clark and Madison Streets, waiting for the superb gold chariot drawn by twenty milk white steeds, and containing fifty musicians, to come along. "Just because she lived in the dark ages," said he, "she is cracked up for a great poet; but she will never be as popular with the masses of Western readers as Ella Wheeler and Marion Harland are. All of her works that remain to us are a few fragments, and they are chestnuts; for they have been printed within the last ten years in the books of a great many poets I could name, and I have read them. We know very little of Sappho's life. If she had amounted to much, we would not be in such ignorance of her doings. The probability is that she was a society or fashion editor on one of the daily papers of her time, a sort of Clara Belle woman, whose naughtiness was mistaken for a species of intellectual brilliancy. Sappho was a gamey old girl, you know. Her life must have been a poem of passion, if there is any truth in the testimony of the authorities who wrote about her several centuries after her death. In fact, these verses of hers that are left indicate that she was addicted to late suppers, to loose morning gowns, to perfumed stationery, and to hysterics. It is ten to one that she wore flaming bonnets and striking dresses; that she talked loud at the theatres and in public generally; and that she chewed gum, and smoked cigarettes, when she went to the races. If that woman had lived in Chicago, she would have been tabooed."

The amiable gentleman who reads manuscripts for Rand, McNally & Co. says that Sappho's manuscripts were submitted to him a year ago. "I looked them over, and satisfied myself that there was nothing in them; and I told the author so. He seemed inclined to dispute me, but I told him I reckoned I understood pretty well what would sell in our literary circles and on our railroad trains."

But while there was a pretty general disposition to criticise Sappho, there was only one opinion as to the circus parade; and that was complimentary. For the nonce, we may say, the cares and vexations of business, of literature, of art, and of science, were put aside; and our populace abandoned itself to a hearty enjoyment of the brilliant pageant which appealed to the higher instincts. And, as the cage containing the lions rolled by, the shouts of the enthusiastic spectators swelled above the guttural roars of the infuriate monarchs of the desert. Men waved their hats, and ladies fluttered their handkerchiefs. Altogether, the scene was so exciting as to be equalled only by the rapturous ovation which was tendered Mdlle. Hortense de Vere, queen of the air, when that sylph like lady came out into the arena of Forepaugh's great circus tent last evening, and poised herself upon one tiny toe on the back of an untamed and foaming Arabian barb that dashed round and round the sawdust ring. Talk about your Sapphos and your poetry! Would Chicago hesitate a moment in choosing between Sappho and Mdlle. Hortense de Vere, queen of the air? And what rhythm be it Sapphic, or choriambic, or Ionic a minore is to be compared with the symphonic poetry of a shapely female balanced upon one delicate toe on the bristling back of a fiery, untamed palfrey that whoops round and round to the music of the band, the plaudits of the public, and the still, small voice of the dyspeptic gent announcing a minstrel show "under this canvas after the performance, which is not yet half completed?"

If it makes us proud to go into our bookstores, and see thousands upon thousands of tomes waiting for customers; if our bosoms swell with delight to see the quiet and palatial homes of our cultured society overflowing with the most expensive wall papers and the costliest articles of virtue; if we take an ineffable enjoyment in the thousand indications of a growing refinement in the midst of us, vaster still must be the pride, the rapture, we feel when we behold our intellect and our culture paying the tribute of adoration to the circus. Viewing these enlivening scenes, why may we not cry in the words of Sappho, "Wealth without thee, Worth, is a shameless creature; but the mixture of both is the height of happiness"?

Eugene Field – A Short Biography

Eugene Field was born on 2nd September, 1850 in St. Louis, Missouri at 634 S. Broadway to parents Roswell Martin and Frances Reed Field, both of New England stock. Tragically Field lost his mother at age 6 and was thereafter brought up by a cousin, Mary Field French, in Amherst, Massachusetts.

Field attended Williams College in Williamstown, Massachusetts.

When he was 19 his father died, and Field dropped out of Williams. Field's father, Roswell Martin Field, was the lawyer for Dred Scott, the slave who famously sued for his freedom. The complaint was sometimes referred to as 'The lawsuit that started the Civil War'.

Field then went to Knox College in Galesburg, Illinois, but again dropped out. This time after a year. However he did then summon himself to attend the University of Missouri in Columbia, Missouri, where his brother Roswell was studying. As can be gathered from his efforts to date Field was not the most serious of students but was gaining the reputation of being a prankster. Among his more outlandish attempts were a raid on the president's wine cellar, painting the president's house in school colors, and firing the school's landmark cannons at midnight.

Field tried acting but found it not to his liking, studied law but with little success, but did have an interest in writing for the student newspaper.

When his studies finished in 1871, although he never graduated, he collected his share of his inheritance from his father's estate, and set off for a trip to explore Europe. After six months, with funds from the inheritance exhausted, he returned to the United States.

Field then set to work as a journalist for the St. Joseph Gazette in Saint Joseph, Missouri, in 1875.

That same year he married the sixteen-year-old Julia Sutherland Comstock of St Joseph, Missouri. They would eventually have eight children during their twenty-two years of marriage, of whom only five would reach adulthood. Field, knowing that his understanding of finances was somewhat poor, arranged for all the money he earned to be sent to his wife for her to administer on behalf of the family.

In his career as a journalist he soon found a niche that suited him. His articles were light, humorous and written in a personal and gossipy style that endeared him to his readership. Some were soon being syndicated to other newspapers around the States. Field rose to be the city editor of the Gazette.

From 1876 through 1880, the Family lived in St. Louis. Field worked initially as an editorial writer for the Morning Journal and then for the Times-Journal. From there he worked for a short time as the managing editor of the Kansas City Times before settling, for two years, as the editor of the Denver Tribune. He also wrote a column for the paper, 'Odds and Ends,' poking fun at the climate, the muddy roads, the frontier language, and other aspects of Denver life. However his readership was large and growing. Further opportunities would come.

In 1883 the Field moved the family to Chicago lured by a salary of $50 a week. Field now began work for the Chicago Daily News. Here he wrote his humorous newspaper column called Sharps and Flats. He quickly found out that $50 dollars in Denver didn't stretch that far in bustling Chicago.

His column ran in the newspaper's morning edition. In it Field made quips about issues and personalities of the day, especially regarding the arts and literature. His pet subject was the intellectual superiority of Chicago, especially when he compared it to Boston, which he often did. In April 1887, he wrote, "While Chicago is humping herself in the interests of literature, art and the sciences, vain old Boston is frivoling away her precious time in an attempted renaissance of the cod fisheries."

In another article that year after Chicago's National League baseball club sold future baseball Hall of Famer Mike "King" Kelly to Boston which overlapped with a speaking tour visit from the famous Boston poet and diplomat James Russell Lowell he wrote: "Chicago feels a special interest in Mr. Lowell at this particular time because he is perhaps the foremost representative of the enterprising and opulent community which within the last week has secured the services of one of Chicago's honored sons for the base-ball season of 1887. The fact that Boston has come to Chicago for the captain of her baseball nine has reinvigorated the bonds of affection between the metropolis of the Bay state and the metropolis of the mighty west; the truth of this will appear in the mighty welcome which our public will give Mr. Lowell next Tuesday."

It was in 1888 that his poem 'Little Boy Blue' was printed in America, a weekly journal. It achieved for Field instant and lasting fame. Coincidentally the same issue carried a poem by James Russell Lowell. Field was immensely pleased that his own poem was regarded with considerably more weight and acclaim.

Field had first published poetry in 1879, when his poem 'Christmas Treasures' was published. It later appeared in 'A Little Book of Western Verse' (1889). This was the beginning that would eventually number over a dozen volumes. He developed a style of light-hearted poems for children. Among the perennial favorites are 'Wynken, Blynken, and Nod' and 'The Duel' (but better known as 'The Gingham Dog and the Calico Cat') and 'Little Boy Blue' about the death of a child. As well as verse Field published an extensive range of short stories including 'The Holy Cross' and 'Daniel and the Devil.'

Field treasured rare, unusual and beautiful books and his personal library had scores of them. He also enjoyed making them too and frequently worked long hours with great care and various colored inks decorating the first letter of his poems.

In 1889 whilst the family were in London and Field himself was recovering from a bout of ill health he wrote his most famous poem; 'Lovers Lane'. It is often thought to have been written whilst the couple were courting but recent research settles it authorship to this later date. The poem was written as a reminder of better days when the couple courted in her father's buggy on 'Lover's Lane, St Jo'.

Field was ever curious and keen to push his boundaries. In 1891 with his brother Roswell they wrote and published 'Echoes from the Sabine Farm' a loosely translated version of Horace.

On 4th November 1895 Eugene Field Sr died in Chicago of a heart attack at the age of 45. He is buried at the Church of the Holy Comforter in Kenilworth, Illinois.

The New York Times described his death: CHICAGO, Nov. 4. — Eugene Field, the poet and humorist, died at 5 o'clock this morning of heart disease at his residence in Buena Park. Although Mr. Field had been ill for the past three days, his sudden death was totally unexpected.

Field was originally interred at Graceland Cemetery in Chicago, but his son-in-law, Senior Warden of the Church of the Holy Comforter, had him reinterred on 7th March, 1926.

Several of his poems were set to music with commercial success. Many of his works were accompanied by paintings from the exceptional talents of Maxfield Parrish.

During his lifetime he was often referred to as the 'poet of childhood'. This may account for his anonymous publication of 'Only a Boy'. In our own times the work would probably be frowned upon. It concerns a 12-year-old boy being seduced by a woman in her 30s. The 1920's drama critic/magazine editor George Jean Nathan claimed it was a popular but forbidden work among those coming of age in the early 1900's.

Much of what Field wrote was light, humourous and of its time. And that is perhaps why it has endured. Its writes of a time that, in his words, suspends itself from the harsh reality of real life to a gentler and more touching time that exists in the imagination.